Agnolo Firenzuola

Tales of Firenzuola, Benedictine monk of Vallambrosa, XVIth

Century

For the first time translated into English

Agnolo Firenzuola

Tales of Firenzuola, Benedictine monk of Vallambrosa, XVIth Century
For the first time translated into English

ISBN/EAN: 9783337072209

Printed in Europe, USA, Canada, Australia, Japan

Cover: Foto ©Andreas Hilbeck / pixelio.de

More available books at **www.hansebooks.com**

TALES

OF

FIRENZUOLA

Benedictine Monk of Vallambrosa
(XVIth CENTURY)

—For the first time translated into English—

PARIS
ISIDORE LISEUX
1889

PREFACE

FIRENZUOLA is more than a pleasing storyteller: he is a masterly writer who adapts a nervous style to the service of a naturally voluptuous imagination, and the pictures of which are of a colouring sparkling with vivacity. He has been praised for his not having adhered to the language such as Dante, Boccaccio, and Petrarch had formed it, and for having enriched his own, with a host of picturesque expressions gathered at the fountain head, namely, borrowed from the ordinary manner of speaking. We hear at Florence as in Paris more tropes on one market day, than during several hundred Academical sittings. His somewhat considerable work comprises a collection of Oriental Apologues entitled : *Discorsi degli Animali; Ragionamenti d'amore;* two *Discourses on Women's Beauty;* two comedies, *La Triunzia* and *I Lucidi;* a translation of the *Golden Ass,* by Apuleius ; poetry in which *Capitoli* slightly sketched and a few desultory pieces, appear. One of them, *Expulsion of new characters uselessly introduced into the Tuscan tongue,* is directed against the Trissino, who wanted to add to the alphabet certain parasitic letters, among others the omega. Two of these works at least were formerly turned into French and seem to have been in great vogue ; the *Discorsi degli Animali* were translated for the first time by Gabriel Cottier, under this heading : *Pleasant and jocose discourses of Animals, with a story not less true than funny lately taken place in the city of Florence,* Lyons, 1556, 16mo, and a second time by Pierre de Larivey ; they form part of a treatise entitled : *Two Books of Fabulous Philosophy,* Lyons, 1579, 16mo. Brantôme was acquainted with the *Discorsi delle bellezze delle donne,* or with the French translation. *The Golden Ass* presents this striking feature that Firenzuola, in substituting himself for the Lucius of Apuleius,

appropriated to himself not only the author's inventions, but also the hero's mis-
haps which he takes on his own account,
and this affords him the opportunity of
recounting to us up to the end, a smattering
of his own biography and a regular genea-
logy of his whole family. Paul Louis Cour-
ier, a shrewd judge of these matters, highly
appreciated this translation owing to its
slightly arch savour. 'Without reproducing
obscure sentences,' says he, 'the forgotten
terms of Fra Jacopone or of Cavalcanti,
Firenzuola borrows from the old Tuscan a
host of ingenuous and charming expressions,
and his version, in which we may say all
the flowers of this admirable language are
concentrated, is, in many persons' opinion,
what is most finished in Italian prose.'

The *Ragionamenti d'Amore* commend
themselves by the same agreeableness of
style and, moreover, the Romances for
which they serve as frame are so many
short masterpieces of sprightly narrative
and ingenious wit. This is evidently his
most vivid creation, the one which assures
him the greatest chance of being known
outside of Italy. Yet they have never
before been turned into English, perhaps

owing to their title, which does not promise
much interest ; perhaps because of the too
refined insipidness of the preliminaries,
which but little lead us to suspect how
much boldness and fantasy the author is
about to display. In imitation of Boccaccio,
Firenzuola supposes that a society of young
ladies and gallant knights is united in a
pleasant villa ; they spend the time in prolonged chattings which by their object recall the quintessenced abstractions of the
Courts of Love, and, having, about night-
fall, chosen a Queen, they relate one after
another merry tales in which, by a satirical
contrast, the heavenly Venus, so mystically
exalted during the preliminaries, is sacrifi-
ced without the least hesitation to the
earthly Venus. Perhaps this is a symbol-
ical turning adopted by the author to make
us comprehend that pure and ideal love,
though excellent as a topic of conversation,
is no longer current in real life.

However witty this frame may be, it does
not possess originality enough to claim
much of our attention ; we have therefore
overlooked the metaphysical discussions at
the beginning of the *Ragionamenti* and
translated only the Romances which form

their conclusion. We shall give a sufficient
idea of the whole in stating that the scene
is laid at Pozzolatico, near Florence, within
the prescribed decorations of this sort of
semi-allegorical compositions : terraced gardens, plashing fountains, purling streams,
shady groves, meadows decked with flowers,
and that the interlocutors are six in number, three gentlemen : Celso, Folchetto,
Selvagio, and three ladies : Costanza Amaretta, Fioretta, and Bianca. Celso is Firenzuola himself ; he assumes this title in
many other works of his ; he appears to
have designated, under the names of Fioretta and Bianca, his sister and sister-in-law ;
under that of Folchetto, Bianca's husband,
his own brother, Girolamo Firenzuola. As
to Costanza Amaretta, who is taken as
Queen, she was a Florentine of high descent
and great wit whom Firenzuola loved with a
tender love, and she died young, in the full
splendour of her beauty. He conserved for
her a kind of worship and, in his *Epistola
in lode delle donne*, addressed to a learned
Sienese, Claudio Tolomei, after having
placed her for her talents and beauty in
the same rank as the most illustrious of
whom ancient or modern history makes

mention—Sappho, Aspasia, Cornelia, Calpurnia, Sempronia, the Marchioness of Pescara, etc., he compares her for virtues to Plato's Diotima, to Saint Monica, the mother of Saint Augustin. But notwithstanding the aureola of chastity with which he piously surrounds her form, he fails not to let her hear with attentive ear a series of tales the principal features of which would disfigure neither the *Moyen de Parvenir*, nor the *Dames Galantes* of Brantôme.

It has been asked whether it is quite true, as some of the ancient titles have it, that the author of these amusing tales and of the *Capitoli* which are not less so, had ever worn the Benedictine habit. Tiraboschi seriously doubts it, for the convincing reason that if Firenzuola was a monk he would have known how to keep a stricter guard over his imagination. The argument is a queer one : the same as if somebody said that Rabelais must not have been Parish Priest of Meudon, since he wrote *Gargantua* and *Pantagruel*. Firenzuola lived and died a Benedictine. Indeed Canon Moreni discovered in the *Bullarium Archiepiscopale* of Florence a brief of Clement VII, dated 1526, annulling his monastic vows, under

the pretext that his ,taking the habit and
his profession were not according to the
rules ; but another act much later on, passed at Prato in 1539, shows us ' the Reveren-
dus Dom Angelus Florentiola, usufructuary
and perpetual Administrator of the Abbey
San Salvator of Vaiano, of the order of Val-
lombrosa,' constituting his brother, Girolamo Firenzuola, as procurator of the Convent. He had therefore remained always
attached to the order, in spite of this annulling brief, which cannot be explained.
Moreover, the *Ragionamenti* are previous to
it ; Firenzuola, who had nothing printed
during his lifetime, dedicated them in 1525
to the Marquis of Camerino, and, still more,
he had read the first Day's Work, the only
one he achieved, to Clement VII, who ex-
pressed himself highly pleased with it. We
have in respect of this the author's own
testimony : ' I will and may boast of this,
that the judicious ear of Clement the sev-
enth, whose praises no quill however good
it be could sufficiently trace, in presence of
the greatest minds of Italy, remained wide
open several hours listening to the sound of
my own voice, while I was reading to him
the *Expulsion of Letters* and the first Day's

Work of these *Ragionamenti*, which I have just dedicated to the Most Illustrious Signora Caterina Cibo, very honourable Duchess of Camerino.'

This remembrance recalled to him the moment of his highest favour in the Pontifical Court. Let us give a few facts of his biography. He was born at Florence in 1493, of a family from Firenzuola, a small town at the foot of the Alps, between Florence and Bologna, whence its ascendants had taken the name. His great-grandfather and grandfather filled important offices in the house of the Medicis; his father, Sebastiano Firenzuola, being successively judge and public notary, discharged the functions of Chancellor, appointed by election as overseer of the city magistrates. His mother was the daughter of Alesandro Braccasi, an estimable scholar, the author of a good translation of Appian, and he was moreover first secretary of the Republic under the grand Dukes Lawrence and Peter de Medicis; he died at Rome, as ambassador of Florence with Alexander VI; Firenzuola got a mausoleum erected to him within the basilic of the Convent of Saint Praxedes, of which he was once an abbot.

Destined by his family to the ecclesiastical state, he went to study canon law at Siena, then at Perugia, where he became acquainted with the famous Pietro Aretino and formed lasting relations with him. These studies shocked him ; he complains somewhere of being consumed in them with great pains and without any pleasure the best part of his youth. He attained nevertheless to a doctor's degree and at once betook himself, about the year 1516, to Rome, where he was attached to the Curia. Under the pontificate of Clement VII, several documents being found by his biographers mark him out as entrusted with the defence of a certain number of cases, in the capacity of procurator, and invested at the same time with the titles of abbot of Saint Praxedes and Saint Mary the Hermit, of Spoleto. Although he had nothing printed, his manuscript works were sufficiently scattered about to win him a lawful renown. He was besides a man of jovial humour, esteemed for the amenity of his character. 'You will diffuse mirth into the souls of those who familiarly frequent you,' writes to him the divine Aretino. 'Remember how I knew you as a schoolboy at Perugia,

as a citizen of Florence, as a prelate in
Rome.' In another letter he reminds him
of his kind turns with the Pope. 'I have
still a recollection of the great pleasure
which Pope Clement felt, the evening I
prevailed on him to read what you had
just composed on the *Omegas* of the Trissino. It was this that determined His
Holiness, at the same time as Monsignor
Bembo, to be eager to know you in person.'
We have seen further back Firenzuola reading to the Pope not only his witty diatribe
against the Trissino, but also the first Day's
Work of the *Ragionamenti;* the Popes of
that time listened to wanton tales, attended
performances of Machiavelli's *Mandragola,*
or Cardinal Bibbiena's *Calandra*, and laughed as simple mortals.

The death of Clement VII, in 1534, the
disgust which Firenzuola felt for his jurid-
ical functions and especially a pernicious
fever, the famous fever of the Pontine
Marshes, which sometimes renders a stay
in Rome very dangerous, obliged him to
abandon the Curia. He obtained the Abbey of Vaiano, near Cremona, but tarried
especially either at Florence or Prato, and
endeavoured to establish in a more whole-

some air his ruined health. The fever was a long while about yielding up; it worked upon him during seven whole years, after having worn him down to a skeleton. 'I had become of so livid a hue, that I looked like a Sienese lately returned from the Maremma. Ah! wretched man! had I fallen asleep at church among the monks, they would have taken me for one who was dead, and have buried me. I absorbed a whole chemist's shop, and had more clysters administered to me than the Bishop of Scala, when he was in the world. I think I broke two hundred chamber-pots, first in Rome, next at Florence, and quite wore out the greatest physicians.'

In fine, he got rid of it thanks only to a decoction of guaiacum, the ' holy wood' so famous in the sixteenth century for its curative virtues. Being grateful, Firenzuola extolled its praises in one of his best Capitoli, *In lode del legno santo,* to which the preceding quotation belongs. Yet his death came on in 1544 or 1545, having closely followed the establishment of his health. He had at least, like the patient of whom a wag of a doctor spoke, the consolation of dying cured. He had the imprudence of

returning to Rome, and he was buried near
his father, within the church of his ancient
Abbey of Saint Praxedes.

This long sickness is perhaps the reason
why the *Ragionamenti d'amore*, his chief
work, remained unfinished.   They were
published, such as they were, with a few
others of his works, by his brother Girolamo,
under the following heading : *Prose di M.
Agnolo Firenzuola, Fiorentino; in Fiorenza,
appresso Lorenzo Torrentino, impressor duc-
ale*, 1552.   Firenzuola intended to add five
more, arranged after the same plan, to the
first Day's Work, composed of preliminary
conversations and six romances.   Later on
they found among his papers four more
romances, matter prepared beforehand for
one of the subsequent Day's Work.   In this
translation they come under the numbers
V, VI, VII, and VIII.   We give the whole
ten in the order adopted by the former
editors, who modified Firenzuola's arrangement in order to make the ten recitals fit
into the frame of but one Day's Work.
Such as they are, these tales give pleasure
by their free allure, their jovial tone, and
the perfect finish of their style, far more
than by the idle dissertations and chattings

which serve them as transitions or entries
into the matter; they cause us to deeply
regret that the author has not written
more of them.

ROMANCE I

The Comely Slave

THERE LIVED IN THIS COUNTRY
LONG AGO, TWO YOUNG MEN OF
high descent, amply supplied with the gifts
of Fortune, who, not content with the val-
iant exploits of their ancestors and not
deeming the actions of others as genuine
illustrations, rendered themselves famous
and recommendable by their own, so that
they imparted more splendour to their
nobleness than they had received from it.
They had, by their cultivated minds, court-
esy and thousand occupations in which
they were engaged, acquired so high a renown in Florence, that he who could speak
most in their praise was deemed indeed
happy. What was especially praiseworthy
in them, was a certain tender friendship, a
certain brotherly love which so united

them that when one went anywhere, the other went with him, and the desire of the one was likewise the desire of the other.

While these young men were thus living an honourable and quiet life, Fortune had, you would say, begrudged them it. For so it turned out that one of the two friends, Niccolo degli Albizzi, had tidings of an uncle's death on his mother's side, a rich merchant of Valencia who, without son or nearer kin, had appointed him his sole heir. It then devolved on Niccolo, who wanted to see his own affairs in person, to make up his mind about going to Spain, and he invited Coppo (this was the other's name) to accompany him, an invitation which was most welcome to him. They had already fixed the day and way of travelling, when their misfortune or doubtless their good luck would have it that just at the time of starting, Coppo's father (Giambatt-ista Canigiani) was stricken by so frightful a sickness that he departed this life for the next in a couple of hours. Now, if Niccolo wanted to set out, he must go alone. He said goodbye to his friend most reluctantly, especially under such trials; but forced by sheer necessity, he set out towards Genoa and, having taken a berth on a Genoese vessel, had the anchor weighed at once. Fortune was most averse to his voyage. He had not yet got more than a hundred miles from land when about sunset the sea, becoming all at once foam, began to rise and threaten, by a thousand signs, imminent danger to the passengers. The captain, wishing to take his precautions, accordingly prepared for it in the greatest hurry; but the rain and wind came suddenly on with so much violence that nothing of what was necessary could be done. Again, the night fell in an instant so pitchy dark that they could no longer distinguish any object on earth, save when a flash of lightning occasionally broke to make the situation still more horrible and dreadful, which plunged everything anew into the most profound darkness. What a pity to behold those poor passengers so often performing precisely what they should not, while they were also trying to meet the threats of heaven! Should the captain give any commands, nobody heard him, because of the rain falling in torrents, the roaring of billows dashing against one another, the straining of cordage, the flapping of sails, the flashing of lightning, and the thunder's roar; the greater the necessity, the more need all had of common sense and courage. What courage could these poor creatures have, in your opinion, on seeing the ship now apparently attempting to jump up to the sky, then cleaving the billows as if with the intent of flinging herself into hell ? Do you fancy their hair stood on end, when it looked as though the firmament, having turned into water, wanted to drop into the sea ; then that the sea, in swelling, wanted to fly to the assault ? What hope do you fancy they had when they beheld the others cast into the deep what they held most preciously, when they flung therein their wealth to avoid themselves a worse destiny ? The vessel dislocated, abandoned to the mercy of the winds, now tossed about by them, now shattered by the waves, all filled with water, was going in search of some rock to put an end to the toils of the unhappy seamen ; these not knowing henceforth what to do, threw themselves into one another's arms, embraced, sobbed, and cried for mercy with all their might. Oh ! how many among them would have liked to console the others, who were themselves in need of consolation and whose voice was smothered with sighs and tears ! Oh ! how many among them, but a little while before, defied heaven, and now seemed nuns at prayers ! Who implored the Virgin Mary, who Saint Nicholas de Bari, who yelled after Saint Elm, who talked of going to the Holy Sepulchre, who of turning monk, and who of taking a wife for God's sake ? Such a merchant swears to make restitution, another to cease usuary ; one calls upon his father, another his mother ; this one recollects his friends, that one his children. What rendered the common calamity a thousand times more horrible was to see the misery of the one taking pity on the other, to hear all these bewailings. While the unhappy creatures were in this painful situation, the topmast was broken off by a sudden sally of the tempest, and the vessel smashed into a thousand pieces, despatched the greater number of the passengers into the dread deep, there to fill the maws of fish and other marine beasts. The remainder, more skilful or less ill-used by Fortune, provided for their safety by holding on to planks. Niccolo had, among the latter, grasped a plank which he

only let go when it landed him on the coast
of Barbary, near Sousa, a few miles from
Tunis. Cast in this place and discovered
by I know not how many fishermen who
had come thither afishing, his state moved
them to pity. They took him up, carried
him off to a cabin hardby, and, having
lighted a big fire, placed him close to it.
After they had with great pain restored
him to his senses and got him to talk, they
noticed he spoke Latin, from which they
rightly concluded he must be a Christian.
and without further thoughts of taking a
better fish for that morning, they unanim-
ously agreed to take him to Tunis, where
they sold him as a slave to a powerful
country gentleman, named Hajji Akhmet.
The latter, seeing the newcomer was young
and goodlooking, thought of keeping him
in his own service, and Niccolo showed so
many proofs of cleverness and diligence in
his duties, that he endeared himself in a
very short time to his master and the whole
household. He became especially a favor-
ite with Akhmet's wife, one of the most
courteous, genteel and comely women that
had ever been or were still on those shores.
He pleased her so well that she was no

longer happy day or night except when she
saw him or heard him speaking; and she
knew so nicely how to get round her husband, who would have imagined anything
else but what really was her object, that he
made her a present of him, so that she
might keep him in her own service. The
lady was most highly delighted at this, and
she curbed her amorous flames for a long
while. Her intention at first was to feed
them in secret, without Niccolo's knowing
anything about it; but from being constantly in his company they grew so troub-
lesome that she was forced to satisfy them
one way or another, and she had more than
once the intention of disclosing her passion
to him. Now, every time she was about
putting her project into execution, the
shame of being in love with a slave, the
dread of not being able to rely on him, the
great dangers to which she saw she was ex-
posing her honour and life, suddenly baffled
her. Retiring frequently alone, fired in
different senses, she used to say to herself:
' Extinguish then, O foolish one, extinguish
then this flame, while only as yet it begins
to kindle ! At present a little water will
do for it, but later on, if it gains ground

over thee, all the water in the sea will not
suffice. Ah! blind woman that thou art,
dost thou not consider the infamy thou
wilt heap on thyself if ever anyone comes
to know that thou hast bestowed thy love
upon a stranger, a slave, a Christian?
Thou wilt no sooner have let him see one
glimpse of liberty, than he will profit by
the occasion to fly away and abandon thee.
O miserable one, to bewail thy folly! Dost
thou not know that while thought is wandering, love can have nothing stable? How
couldst thou expect to be loved by him who
dreams only of gaining his liberty? With-
draw from this nonsensical undertaking,
let thy foolish love vanish, and if thou wilt
at any price stain thy honesty, let it be in
favour of someone who will not be here-
after a subject of shame to thee, that thou
mayest excuse thyself in the eyes of those
who may have heard of thy imprudence.
But to whom am I speaking, O unfortunate
one? to whom am I addressing such sup-
plications? How could I have a will of my
own, I, who belong to another? These
thoughts, these projects, these deliberations
do not become thee, O wedded wife, but
rather those who can dispose of themselves

as they please; they do not become one
who is in the power of a man as I am; I
must turn my ear to the side where the
voice of the master calls me. Turn then,
O foolish one, turn thy words to better use,
lose time no longer, waste thyself away no
more. What thou wilt not do today, thou
shalt be forced to do tomorrow, while running the greatest risks. Try that thy lover's will become one and the same with thy
own, and know that, stranger as he is, he
ought not to be held the less estimable for
that, either by thee or anybody else. If we
were to set a high price only on the pro-
ductions of our own country, I cannot see
why gold, pearls and other precious objects
should be of so great a value, as they really
are, outside the countries which produce
them. Fortune has made a slave of him,
but she has not on that account robbed him
of his pleasant manners; nor does it hinder
me from recognizing the greatness of his
soul, from beholding the splendor of his
merits. Fortune alters nothing at birth;
it may betide anybody to become a slave;
it is not his fault, it is Fortune's; therefore
I ought to despise Fortune, and not him.
And if it befell me to become a slave, it

would not make me, in the bottom of my
soul, other than I am. Let not then these
motives prevent my wishing him well; is
it because he belongs to another religion,
that I should be the more averse to him?
Well, what of that, O foolish one! Am I
more certain of my religion than of his?
Supposing I had a thousand times all the
certainty in the world about it, I do not
deny it on that account, I do not the
slightest thing contrary to our gods; yet
who knows if, loving and beloved by him,
I shall not prevail over him to believe in
our law? I shall thus perform an act at
once agreeable to myself and our gods.
Why struggle against myself and be an
enemy to my own pleasures? Why not
obey my own inclinations? Do I fancy
myself able to resist the laws of love?
What innocence of soul were mine if I, who
am but a poor silly woman, the frail target
of Cupid's darts, should think myself able
to keep on my guard against what thou-
sands of the wisest of men could not escape!
Let my passion then triumph over every
other consideration, let the feeble force of
a tender young woman no longer try to
struggle against that of so powerful a mas-

ter ! '

After the enamoured woman had many
times reasoned and fought with herself,
she finally ceded the victory to the one of
the two sides towards which Love had,
thanks to her own good will, urged her;
and no sooner had she imagined a chance
for it, than she drew Niccolo aside, told him
of her torments and pleaded for his love.
Niccolo was quite bewildered at first on
hearing the like, and all sorts of fancies
whirled through his brain. He feared she
acted in this way only to put him to the
test, and he had half a mind to make her
an ill-boding answer ; but the remembrance
of certain fondlings she used to bestow on
him rushed back into his head, and because
he had discovered more discretion in her
than the women of that country usually
have, he bethought him of the romance of
the Count of Antwerp and of the Queen of
France, besides a thousand other like in-
stances, and he deemed the occasion propitious, whatever should become of it, to
reply that he was wholly disposed to obey
her behest ; which he did. Nevertheless,
whether he acted thus to give the thing a
higher relish, whether he wished to make

somewhat of a trial of himself, or in fine no
matter why, he kept her many days in sus-
pense before deciding on it. And when she,
who desired something else than empty
words, clapped the saddle on his back, as
the saying is, he who saw by a thousand
signs that he was her master, resolved to
make a Christian of her to further his own
ends, before satisfying her.   By means of
fair and well prepared words he told her
how he was at her command, but that he
entreated her beforehand to promise that
she would do him a very easy thing which
he would ask of her.   The woman, on whom
the time weighed like a thousand years
until the final putting of the business into
operation, without thinking what he could
want and out of her wits through so ardent
a desire, pledged him her faith and swore a
thousand oaths to do whatever he should
request, whereupon Niccolo gently explained to her the nature of his resolution.
At first the imposed condition seemed very
hard to the poor creature, and were it not,
as she incessantly repeated, that she was
ever doomed to follow the will of another,
I doubt not but that she would have refus-
ed to commit this folly.   But Love, who is

so well accustomed to perform miracles, knew too how to persuade her, so that after many hesitations and excuses, she was forced to say : ' Do with me as you please.' Thus, to cut a long story short, on the same day she received baptism, on the same day they were betrothed, on the same day they consummated their marriage, and the mysteries of this new religion seemed so sweet to her that, after the example of Alibech, she constantly upbraided herself for having so long delayed making a trial of it. She loved so well to be within its embrace and thoroughly instructed therein, that she no longer had any happiness except when inculcating on herself some new doctrine.

While Niccolo was teaching, she learning, and while they were both at so mild a school, without anybody getting the slightest clue into the secret, Niccolo's friend Coppo had had knowledge of his adventure and had, with a most resolute idea of effecting his ranson, come with a large sum of money to the coast of Barbary. He arrived at Tunis, and had hardly landed when he men Niccolo who was haply returning from I know not where with his mistress. After they had recognized each other, not without difficulty, and embraced and kissed at least a thousand times, Niccolo, the moment he had learnt the object of his voyage and offered him becoming thanks, forbade him to hint a word about his ransom until they should talk over it again, for a reason which he explained to him later on. He then pointed out a place where they could see each other the next day and, without further discourse, took leave of him. The wife wanted to know at once who that man was and what conversation they had together, for she was torn by jealousy, fearing that not only any person whatever but even the bird flitting through space, might carry off her dear lover. He managed to satisfy her by means of a few stories of his own making. Niccolo had, as anyone may easily imagine, a very great desire for returning home; but knowing for certain that if his passionate young wife discovered anything about it, she would utterly ruin him or at least undermine his projects, he wavered at attempting the slightest thing whatever, and this was the reason why he did not wish Coppo to hint a word about it to anybody. For my part I think that this love, being deeply rooted within his heart from long habit, for you are well aware that

Love dispenses no man beloved fron loving:

would have placed before his eyes so many perils and obstacles that he would have resigned himself to stay where Fortune had cast him. He had nevertheless sense enough to see that this woman was allowing herself to be carried away by her passion for him, and that Hajji Akhmet would at last find out their secret. For this reason he had thought more than once of sounding her to see whether she would be willing to go to his country, and he saw her so blinded for his sake that he felt sure he would not have much trouble in persuading her, but as he had not yet solved the problem of ways and means he had remained silent until this moment. Now that Coppo was here, and thinking his coming was opportune and that the plan would succeed far more easily, he deemed it necessary to talk it over with his friend before treating about the ransom. Having then found Coppo and having thoroughly examined all the pros and cons of the case, they finally agreed upon what was to be done in the event of the woman consenting.

Niccolo chose a favorable moment and place and, having greeted her, he said: 'My very dear mistress, to think of what it would have been necessary to do oneself, when another has fallen into a misfortune which he might quite at first have avoided, is nothing else than to wish, without knowing anything about it, to show oneself wise after the accident. It therefore appears to me necessary, if we do not wish to be numbered among such persons, to avoid the dangerous defiles into which our love is leading us, before we break our necks. Love has rendered us so reckless that, as you may judge of it still better than I, if we do not remedy it, I feel it will be the cause of our downfall. This is why I have more than once thought to myself of the means we could employ in order to escape from such a danger, and, out of a certain number which I have carefully considered, I can think of but two which are less hard than the rest. The first of them is that we shall give our minds to gradually ending our amatory customs; that way will seem to you, if your ardor is equal to mine, so hard that any other expedient, no matter

how severe, will be comparatively less painful; so, in my mind, the second has always
pleased me better, although it must seem
to you at first very burdensome and difficult
to carry out. Yet I doubt not but that
by force of pondering well over it, you will
finish by finding it smiling invitingly upon
you to decide and choose it boldly. You
shall behold your lover's, your husband's
interest and honor springing therefrom, and
the opportunity of enjoying our love for
ever without anguish of soul and without
peril. My plan is for you to go with me to
our lovely Italy. What a country it is
compared with this, we will leave for future
discussion. Besides, you have often heard
it spoken of before both by me and others.
Florence, the pleasant place of my birth,
is situated in the center. It has the mildest of climates and is, be it said without
disparaging others, surely the finest city in
the whole world. I will not speak of chur-
ches, palaces, private dwellings, streets
s.raight as gun-barrels, fine and spacious
squares, all that is within the walls; why,
the outskirts, the gardens, the villas with
which it is more copiously supplied than
any other city, these will appear to you as

so many paradises, and should God grant
us the grace of arriving there safe, He
knows how happy you will live there, and
how you will upbraid yourself for not having been the first to request it. But let us
lay aside what may be advantageous and
pleasing to you ; I know you set but little
value on that, compared with what is advantageous and pleasing to me ; even
though everything should avert you from
this resolution, would it not suffice, in order to persuade you, to think of the wretched state out of which you would take
your lover, your spouse ? He loves you so
fervently that he prefers to live a bondsman
in a foreign land, he who could live a free-
man in his own, rather than abandon you.
Yes, he could so, for henceforth the means
for redeeming me are not wanting, provided
that the love I bear you permits me to do
as I like with myself. That Christian to
whom I was speaking the other day has
almost come to an understanding with your
husband but, please God, I shall not leave
without my lady, my mistress, my soul !
I know her love for me is so strong, her
confidence in my words so unbounded, that
it seems to me I behold her already fix her

thoughts on this means which to my mind
is the most propitious.   Why do you hesi-
tate ?   What is holding you, Madam, that
I hear you not pronounce, as promptly as
I could have wished, some loving word ?
Perhaps it seems impossible to you to leave
your fatherland ?   If I am your happiness,
as you have a thousand times declared,
where I shall be, will you not have your
country, your spouse, your all ?   The more
you leave behind you here, the more you
shall find over there, even a hundredfold,
and you will be so delighted in frequenting
our ladies, especially one of my little sisters,
that you will think you have left the wild
forests to come and live among men.   This
sister of mine will love and cherish you
dearly when she learns of your kindnesses
to me, and you will surely bless the day
when you arrived in that delightful country.
This is not the time to discuss the merits
of other men with you ; besides, you solved
the question yourself long ago.   Yet, if I
have pleased and still please you to such a
degree that you should bestow on me your
own sweet self, I, who look more like a
countryman than a brave champion, the
more then will the other men be pleasing

to you for they have more graces than I. That which keeps you, now that all other reasons counsel you to fly, would it be the dread of what might be said of you in this country after your departure ? Ah ! Madam, let not that either hinder you from doing what is so advantageous to us both. Not that honor ought not to be placed above all, and I confess the opinion is good of those who claim that we must not mind the evil people say of us, so long as their words do not reach our ears. But neither you nor anybody else ought to be troubled about a reproach wrongfully aimed, as would be your case should anyone reprove you in this. Who can backbite you with righteous teeth for having abandoned the false religion to embrace the true one, because you have fled far from those who are deadly enemies to us Christians ? Who will blame you for having entered the land of your spouse, for having dragged him out of slavery ? nobody of sound judgment. On the contrary there will be a host of persons to congratulate you, to extol you to the skies. Of what are you thinking then, my darling soul ? That which is keeping you back, would it be forsooth the hard-

ship and peril which you know inseparable
from such an enterprise ?   If that is so, I
can assure you there would be little risk ;
whereas to remain here, to conduct ourselves as our mutual love compels us, is
obviously dangerous.   Now, who is there
who would not expose himself to an uncertain peril in order to avoid another which
he knows to be most certain ?   As to the
difficulties, I shall take charge of them myself, and I so swear to you upon my faith,
if God does not deprive me of your favor,
which enables me to live happy even in
bondage.   I have found through that friend
with whom you so often find me convers-
ing, the means of our getting away in all
safety, on one of his vessels.   Consider, my
darling mistress, what confidence I have
placed in you that I should disclose to you
such grave projects.   Reflect on all the
good things we stand to gain, and give no
thought to the dangers and difficulties.
Get ready then to free me from bondage,
get ready to take me to my beloved city,
to your city, to my sister who, with tearful
eyes and outstretched arms, implores you
to restore me to her, and who offers you a
loving welcome.'   He accompanied these

last words with deep-drawn sighs which would have moved the eternal hills, and was then silent.

Niccolo's words so deeply touched the heart of the tender young woman that, although it appeared to her cruel and preposterous to take such a resolution, although she felt a thousand difficulties, a thousand perils pass through her head, she was thinking at the same time of all those perfidies which, they say, you men practice towards women silly enough to love you. Urged on by her great love, which smoothened down for her all the mountains, she, like the courageous women she was, told him without more ado that she was ready to do his will. To cut a long story short, after he had arranged with Coppo the when and the how and had procured the needful supplies, the woman, having previously made provision of a fair share of gold and silver and other valuables, feigned one fine morn to go out for a walk and repaired with Niccolo to the coast where Coppo's ship was moored. The moment they arrived, she and all those who were to cross over pretended they wanted to visit the ship and, leaving the others on shore, embarked and speedily gave the sails to the wind, and before the bystanders were aware of what had happened, the ship was a mile from the shore. When they realized the trick that had been played on them they were amazed and angered, and they straightway imformed Hajji Akhmet. You can imagine what a fuss was made and how everything was done to overtake them, but the wind was so favorable that they had almost reached Sicily before the pursuit began. They landed at Messina because the lady, being but sorrily accustomed to so many fatigues, was in need of rest. They therefore made up their minds to go into the heart of the town and put up at the best hotel they could find, which they did.

Now it chanced that the Court was transferred to Messina during those days, and an ambassador of the king of Tunis having come with the king of Sicily to treat some very weighty affairs, was just staying at the same hotel as our heroes, as ill-luck would have it. He perceived I know not how often the young woman by stealth, so to speak, fancied he knew her and, while remaining thus in doubt, there arrived from his Prince some letters informing him about her flight and ordering him, if she haply landed in that country, to use all his endeavors with the king and those of whom there might be need, to have her brought back to her husband. As soon as had perused the letters, the ambassador held it for certain that this was she, and he went immediately to the king and unfolded to him his Prince's commands. The king without any delay summoned the woman and two young men before him; he had no trouble in perceiving that it was she whom they were looking for and, desirous of doing something pleasing to the king of Tunis, commanded that they should be sent back at once, without any argument. What grief was that of the poor young woman, of her unhappy Niccolo and of Coppo likewise, when they heard such sorrowful news! What cries, what tears, and what prayers! I should never have the heart to relate the thousandth part of them. Taken back by force to the harbour and re-embarked on the same ship, the command of which the king confided to a man on whom he relied, they were conveyed back to Barbary, as prisoners of the king of Tunis. Thanks to more favorable weather than they would have desired, they had already got within a few miles of the creek of Carthagena, when Fortune, tired at last of so many annoyances and toils conjured up against poor Niccolo, resolved to give the wheel a turn. She caused so terrible a wind and tempest to rage that the ship was driven violently back and, within a few hours, the thing is scarcely credible, she was carried into our Tyrrhenian Sea, off Leghorn. Despoiled of her mast and rigging, and quite disabled, she fell into the hands of Pisan corsairs who allowed the young lady and two young men to redeem themselves for a large sum of money, and the three betook themselves to Pisa. They stayed there some time to establish the young lady's health, which was harassed by so many fatigues and chagrins; then, when she looked sufficiently recovered, they set out for Florence. The kind reception, the festivities, the caresses with which they were loaded on their return, I could not imagine, much less describe.

After the young woman had lived a few days in joy, when she had become strong and gay as Niccolo desired, he had her baptised and christened Beatrix. The town made a general holiday of the event.

Niccolo then resolved to get married according to the Christian rite and, that the feast might be complete and the rejoicings general, and that the friendship which united him with Coppo might be bound by still closer ties, he gave him his sister in wedlock, and she, besides being very handsome, was no less virtuous.

The weddings being over, Signora Beatrix, more and more satisfied with the country and the conversation of the men and women, owned that Niccolò had not told her lies. She had so much friendship for her sister-in-law and the latter for her, that it would not have been easy to know which friendship was the most intimate, that of the women or that of the men. The whole four lived together so amicably that all Florence had no other topic for conversation. They became every day more happy, more contented, and more desirous of pleasing one another, nor did familiarity beget weariness in their hearts; far from that, their tenderness increased daily, and they lived a long life of perfect happiness.

ROMANCE II

THE METAMORPHOSIS

There was at Tivoli, an ancient city of
the Latins, a gentleman named Cecc' Antonio Fornari who had the idea of taking a
wife at an age when other men have a thousand griefs from theirs, and, as is the case
with old men, he would not take one unless
she was young and good-looking. He lit
on the right thing.

One of the Coronati, named Giusto, and
a man of some note be it said, seing himself overstocked with a batch of daughters
and so as not to be obliged to hand out a
large dowry, gave the old man one of them,
a pretty and comely lass. She, on seeing
herself tied up to an old fellow fallen back
into childhood, and henceforth deprived of

those pleasures on account of which she had long wished to abandon her home and parents, became very angry about it. She soon grew so disgusted at the spitting, wheezing and other trophies of her husband's old age, that she thought of making herself amends and got it into her head to take, should the occasion present itself, somebody who could supply the wants of her youth better than her father had known how to do.

Fortune was far more propitious to her schemes than she had dared to hope. In fact, a young Roman named Fulvio Macaro, having repaired to Tivoli with his friend Menico Coscia, by way of amusement, and having frequently a glimpse of the young woman who appeared to him pretty, as indeed she was, fell ardently in love with her and, entrusting this Menico with the secret of his love, commended himself to him for his help.

Menico, who was a man to get out of any scrape, told his friend to be of good cheer and that if he was resolved on following out his idea in everything, he well knew how to settle matters in a way which would enable him to be with the young woman as often as he liked. You imagine how Fulvio, who had no other desire, told him thereupon to call on him next day, but Menico replied that he was prepared to go into the matter at once, provided his friend helped. 'I have been told,' said Menico, 'that the lady's husband is on the lookout for a slip of a girl about fifteen for housework, and that he will marry her off at the end of a few years, as is still the custom at Rome. I have determined that it shall be you who will go to him, to remain there as long as you please, but listen awhile how. Our neighbor, that man from Tagliacozzo who comes sometimes to our place to do one thing or another is, as you know, a great friend of mine. While talking to me yesterday about one thing or another, he told me the old fellow had commissioned him to procure the servant, and to do this he was going home in a few days to see if he could find someone there. He is poor, and willingly offers his services to the rich. I feel sure that for a small consideration he would do whatever we wish. Let him then pretend that he has gone to Tagliacozzo and is to return thence in a fortnight or so. He will dress you up like a village girl and,

passing you off for one of his relations, will
place you in your lady's mansion. When
there you will only have yourself to blame,
if your courage fails you. What will help
you in all this is the whiteness of your skin,
your beardlessness, and the fact that you
have a womanish face, which has often
made people think you were a woman
dressed up as a man. Besides, as your
nurse belonged to that village, I think you
will be able to talk like a native.' The
poor lover agreed to all this, and it seemed
to him that he must wait an eternity for
the scheme to be put into execution. In
his imagination he was already with the
lady, helping her with the housework.

Without wasting a single moment the
two friends hurried off to find the countryman who was very glad of the commission,
and they settled beforehand everything
that was to be done. Before a month had
gone by, Fulvio was working as a house-
maid, and he waited on the lady (who was
named Lavinia) so diligently that not only
she but the whole household had the warm-
est regard for him. While Lucia (thus he
had called himself), remaining in this pos-
ition, was waiting for an opportunity of

being serviceable to her otherwise than in making the bed, it happened that Cecc'Antonio went to spend a few days in Rome, and Lavinia, seeing herself left alone, had the whim of taking Lucia to sleep with her.

On the first night, after they had got between the sheets, to one of them all mirthful at the unexpected windfall it seemed a thousand years until the other fell asleep to gather while she slept the fruit of her turmoils, this other thinking of some young blade who was shaking the dust off her fur better than her husband, began to embrace and kiss Lucia most affectionately and, as that may turn out, her hand just strayed towards the side of the place where one distinguishes a boy from a girl. Finding she was not there a woman like herself, she greatly wondered and withdrew her hand to herself, not less astounded than she would have been if she had felt all of a sudden a snake under a tuft of grass. Lucia waited without daring to say or do anything for the issue of the scheme, and Lavinia, doubting that this was the servant, stared as one aghast; yet, seeing that it was indeed Lucia, but not venturing to speak to her, she had the thought of putting her hand again on the object of her astonishment, found it as at first and felt uncertain as to whether she were awake or dreaming. Then thinking that perhaps her touch might be deceiving her, she lifted the clothes, wishing to assure herself of the whole fact with her own eyes. She not only beheld with her eyes what she had touched with her hands, but discovered a heap of snow having the form of a man and the tint of fresh roses, so that she was compelled to admit the evidence, and to believe that so great a change was miraculously wrought that she might safely taste the sweetness of love during the days of her youth. Being quite encouraged, she turned towards Lucia and said: ' Oh ! what do I see there this night with my own doubting eyes ? I know right well that you were just now a girl, and lo ! you are now become a boy. How is that ? 1 fear I see awry or that you are some evil spirit come to my bed instead of Lucia, to make me fall into wicked temptations. Indeed I must see to the bottom of this ! ' While speaking thus, she slipped under Lucia and began to excite her with those provocations which frolicsome girls willingly make use of

on young brats formed before their age.
She assured herself at this game that it was
not a spirit bewitched and that she had
not seen amiss, and she had such comfort
therefrom as you yourself may imagine.

But do not think that she considered
herself as out of doubt the first time, or
even the third. Such mysteries are not to
be accepted lightly, and I can assure you
that if she had not feared for the changing
of the real Lucia into a ghost, she would
have believed herself quite certain of the
fact only at the sixth essay. When this
stage had been reached she passed from
deeds to words and tenderly enquired by
what manner of means the change had
come about. So Lucia, recalling the events
since the first day of her love, related the
whole story to her. Lavinia was exceedingly glad to see herself loved by so pretty
a youth and to know how he had exposed
himself to so many turmoils and perils for
her sake. Passing from this account to
other moving discourses, and perhaps still
wishing to come to a certainty for the sev-
enth time, they tarried so long about getting up that the sun was already peeping
in through the window. The moment for

doing so seemed to them arrived, and after having decided that Lucia should remain a girl during the daytime before everybody, and become a boy at night or whenever they might find the means of being alone, they left the room all joyful.

This happy accord lasted a long while; months passed without anyone in the house becoming aware of anything, and it would have continued so for years had not Cecc' Antonio, although he was as I have said altogether beyond the age, and his donkey could hardly convey the corn to the mill once a month, seeing Lucia tripping about the house and considering her pretty good-looking, bethought himself of wishing to discharge a sieveful into her press, and teased her several times by his importunities. Lucia, fearing that some scandal might result from it one fine day, besought Lavinia for God's sake to rid her of such an annoyance. I have no need to tell you whether the gnat pricked her and whether she hummed a blindman's litany the first time she had an interview with her husband. All I can certify is that she called him something less than lord. 'Look at the bold foot-soldier who wants to go

through his drills like a cavalier! Well I
never! What would you be like if you
were young and jolly? You who have now
to occupy yourself no longer except with
the graveyard and await every moment the
final decree! A pretty smack in the face
you want to give me! Leave, you old fool,
leave sin as it has left you. Do you not
know that even were you steel, you would
not be capable of forming the tip of a Dam-
ascus needle? Oh, it would do you great
honor when you would have reduced this
poor girl, who is as good as bread, to what
I will not name! That will be her dowry,
to serve her for a husband. How pleased
her parents will be! How merry all her
relations will be when they discover they
have entrusted their ewe lamb to the care
of wolves! Tell me briefly, nasty man, if
like was done on yourself, what would you
think about it? What! have you not set
all Paradise in a stir these latter days because I was serenaded? But do you know
what I have to tell you? You will make
me think of things of which I never dreamt
up to now; oh, yes! oh, yes! you shall have
something to make you merry one of these
fine days. Just you wait a bit; I shall put

in your way what you are looking for, and since I understand that by conducting myself well it succeeds but ill with me, I shall now try if conducting myself badly does not succeed better. Whoever will have fair weather in this low deceitful world, has only to do evil!' As she accompanied these last words with four wicked little tears forcibly shed, she affected the old scamp so much that he begged her pardon and promised never to rebuke her again. But his promises were of little value and, if the tears were feigned, so was the relenting which they had provoked.

A few days later, Lavinia having repaired to a wedding party which the people of Tobaldo were celebrating, and having left behind Lucia who felt somewhat indisposed, the enterprising old fellow found her lying asleep. Here was his chance! He slipped his hands underneath her skirts and, lifting them to indulge in his little pleasure, he lighted on what he little expected. Bewildered with wonder, he stood for some time like a lifeless thing; then, revolving a thousand bad thoughts in his head, he began to ask himself what this thing meant. Lucia had her explanations and excuses

quite pat, for she had long ago conferred
thereon with Lavinia in case such a thing
should crop up, and knowing that he was a
jolly old fellow to believe a fib just as well
as the truth ; that he was not so terrible in
reality as he appeared in words ; she did
not in the least trouble herself, and pretended to be shedding bitter tears and implored him to hear her reasons. After he
had encouraged her with a few kind words,
she began, with trembling voice and downcast eyes, to tell her tale. ' Know, my
dear lord, that when I came into this house
(cursed be the hour I put my foot here,
since so silly an adventure was to befall me
in it !) I was not what I am now. Three
months ago (my God, sad life is mine !)
that thing there came to me. One day as
I was washing with lye, I felt a heavy
weariness creep over me, and this began to
grow, so small, so small, then it gradually
began increasing in size so thoroughly that
it has arrived at the degree you see, and if
I had not seen your nephew, the tallest of
them, having one like it, I should have
thought it was some evil growth ; for it
sometimes gives me so much trouble that I
would prefer to have I know not what, I

am so ashamed of it. Yes, indeed, I am so
ashamed of it that I have never dared open
my mouth about it to anybody. Thus
since there is on my part neither fault nor
sin, I beseech you for God's sake and our
Good Lady of Olive, to have pity on me.
I promise you I would rather die than that
people should learn so shameful a thing
about a poor girl such as I.'

The dear old man, who was quite out of
his depth, seeing the tears raining down her
cheeks and hearing her reciting her reasons
so nicely, began almost to believe that she
was speaking the truth. Nevertheless, as
this change seemed almost too much of a
good thing, and recalling the caresses which
Lavinia was wont to lavish on Lucia, he
suspected some underhand work and asked
himself if Lavinia had not, after finding
the thing out, taken advantage of the
windfall right under his very nose. So he
questioned Lucia more explicitly and asked
her whether her mistress knew about it.
'The Lord preserve me!' she boldly replied, seeing that the affair was progressing
favorably; 'I have always been on my
guard against that. I have told you and I
repeat it, I would rather die than anyone

in the world should know it. If God cures me of this evil, no man living except yourself shall know it; and may God grant, since He brought this infirmity on me, that I may return to my former state! To tell you the truth, I am so grieved about it that I am sure to die soon; for besides the shame it will cause me every time I see you, knowing that you know my story, it seems to me I am the most encumbered creature in the world with this thing, excuse my mentioning it, swinging between my legs.' 'Come, my child,' replies old greybeard quite affected, 'remain as you are, and say nothing to anybody; perhaps we may find some medicine to cure you; leave it to me, and on no account say a word to your mistress.'

Thus, without another word, his head in a whirl, he left her and sought out the local doctor, whom they called Master Consolo, and goodness knows how many more people, to enquire about the accident.

Meanwhile Lavinia returned home, and when she had learnt from Lucia what had happened, I leave you to imagine what she felt. I reckon it was sadder news for her than when she knew she had so old a husband. Cecc' Antonio, who had gone, as I have just stated, to enquire about the malady, having heard so much about it in one way or another, returned home more perplexed than ever. Without saying a word to anybody that night, he resolved to set out for Rome the next morning in search of some learned man who knew better how to expound the enigma to him.

At dawn he mounted his horse and proceeded on his way. He alighted at a friend's house and, after a light repast, he repaired to the University, thinking to find there better than elsewhere somebody who would know how to get this flea out of his ear, and by a happy chance he fell precisely on that dear comrade who had got Lucia placed in his household. The young man came sometimes into these quarters for pastime. Our old friend seeing him smartly dressed and saluted by a crowd of people, thought that he must be some great scholar, so he led him aside and, under an oath of secrecy, entrusted him with his torment. Menico, who thoroughly knew the fine old fellow, and who guessed at once how things stood, said to himself while laughing up his sleeve : ' You have put up at the right inn, old pal ;'

and after a long conversation, he gave him
to understand once for all that the thing
was not only possible, but that it had already happened several times. In order
more easily to gain his belief, he took him
to a bookshop and asked for a Pliny in
Italian. He showed him what this author
says about a similar case, Book VII, chap.
IV ; he then showed him what Battisto
Fulgoso writes of it in his chapter ' On
Miracles,' and in this way he tranquilized
the old man's conscience so well that if all
the people in the world had told him different, he would not have believed them.
Once Menico was convinced that the thing
had thoroughly entered the old boy's head
and that it was not likely to leave it, he
struck up another anthem and set out to
persuade him not to send Lucia away from
his house. It was, said he, a good omen
for a place when such accidents came unexpectedly : there was never anything else
but boys, and a thousand other ridiculous
stories. He then begged him so strictly, if
ever he had any doubt to clear up, to apply
always to him, and he would help him most
willingly ; and he knew so well how to give
him reasons, that the good old man would

not have sold them for any amount of money.

After having thanked this learned man and offered him all his fortune, Cecc' Antonio took leave of him. It seemed to him a thousand years before he got back to Tivoli to see if he could beget a boy.

As soon as he got home he began the attempt, and right nobly his wife did her share, so as not to give the lie to the omen. In due course Lavinia was brought to bed of a boy, which meant that Lucia remained at the house as long as she liked, without the old fellow perceiving or wishing to perceive anything,

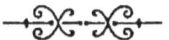

ROMANCE III

THE DOUBLE CHANGE

There lived in the time of our fathers, at Florence, a very rich merchant named Girolamo Cambini who had a wife that was held in her youth to be incontestably the prettiest in the whole town. What was above all the rest praiseworthy in her was her virtue, so much so that she made a show of placing nothing at a higher price, and, far from looking at men, she seemed to be unaware of their existence.

Now it happened that many fellows, after having been smitten by her extraordinary beauty, perceiving at length her coldness and not having been able to obtain from her a single glance, desponded in a short time of the enterprise ; and it was, I think, their complaints, often heaved to heaven, that decided Love to take charge of their vengence.

There lived in Florence at this time a young man of noble family named Master Pietro of the Bardi, but, as he was a priest who possessed among other benefices a fine abbey, people called him the Abbot. He was universally considered the handsomest fellow in Florence, and I think I remember having seen him when I was a slip of a girl, and old as he was then, he still seemed very good-looking. Our charming young wife could not, thanks to that lovely form, prevent herself from making a truce with her hard-heartedness and falling madly in love with him; nevertheless, in order not to wander away from her habits, she enjoyed him and his good looks in the depths of her soul without letting anything come to the surface, or she used to talk of him mysteriously with one of her little chambermaids, bred and fed in her father's house, whom she kept for her personal service. In this way she smothered her amorous flames as best she could.

Many and many days had sped by for her in like sufferings, when at last the idea

struck her to make shift with her amorous
caprice in such a way that neither the Abbot nor anybody else would suspect anything, and here is how. She enjoined on
her maid Laldomine, every time she should
happen to meet the aforesaid Abbot, to
attract his attention by oglings and slight
tokens of friendship, guessing that he would
be easily smitten thereby, the more so because the girl was very pretty, having something alluring in her, and besides, her pec-
uliar garments which were not quite those
of a person of condition nor yet those of a
servant, imparted to her an extraordinary
grace.

One morning as the two women were at
Santa Croce, on the occasion of some feast
or other, the Abbot happened to be there
also, and the cunning little wench put her
mistress's recommendations into practice,
though quite uselessly for the Abbot saw
or feigned to see nothing, probably because
he was still young and unused to such goings-on.

There chanced to be in the Abbot's company another young man, a Florentine also,
named Carlo Sassetti, who, having long
coveted this Laldomine, remarked her ogl-

ings, and set about devising some clever trick; he was only awaiting an opportunity and he immediately put his project into execution.

It so happened about this time that the husband of Agnoletta (such was the lady's name), mounted horse and set out to Florence for a few days. Carlo, who had an eye open for that, used to do nothing but pass every evening between eight and nine o'clock along the street in which the two women were living, and once he perceived Laldomine through a pretty low window on the ground floor, near the staircase looking over a little street which was next the house. Owing to the heat, which was very great, the servant was going with a candle in her her hand to fetch her mistress some water. Carlo had no sooner caught a glimpse of her than he drew near the window and began in a low voice to call Laldomine; she was quite astonished but, instead of closing the window and going about her business as anyone would have done who did not wish to listen to idle stories and answer them, she hid the light, came to the window and said: 'Who is there?' Carlo quickly answered that it was the sweetheart whom

she knew very well, and that he wanted to
have two words with her. 'What sweetheart do you mean? You had better go
about your business, and be ashamed to
you. By God's cross! if our men were
here you would not act like that. A sign
there's no one at home but women! Leave
here, bad luck to you, you brazen scamp,
before I break my jug on your head!'
Carlo, who had been more than once in such
scrapes and knew that the true manner of
saying No is for us not to lend our ears to
the least word of tricksters, was not a bit
frightened. Using the sweetest of accents,
he besought her once more to open the
door, saying at the same time that he was
the Abbot. The wench had no sooner
heard the Abbot named than she softened
down completely, and in a chastened tone
enquired: 'What Abbot? What have I
to do with abbots and monks? Begone,
begone! If you were the Abbot you would
not be out at this time of day; I know very
well that good priests like he is do not ram-
ble about at night a-whoring after other
men's wives, and especially to the homes of
honest women.' 'My Laldomine,' Carlo
replied, 'the great love I bear you forces

me to do what I ought to be on my guard against ; but if I come to importune you at such an hour, let it not surprise you. I have so earnest a desire to open my heart to you, that there is nothing I would not do for the sake of a few words with you. Have then the goodness, my hope, to let me in, if only for a moment ; do not refuse me a thing of such slight importance.'

Laldomine felt touched by such entreaties and, thinking it certainly was the Abbot, she was for opening the door on the instant ; but she thought it would be as well to make sure it really was he by means of some understood sign, so she resolved to wait till the following night. She therefore said to him, half in jest : ' Be off with you, rascal ! Do you think I do not know that you are not the Abbot ? If I were quite sure you were he I would let you in, not to do harm you may be sure, but to find out what you want with me and to tell Girolamo of the fine affronts you offer him when he is not at home. And if you were not the Abbot ? Oh, unhappy woman that I should be ! I should consider myself the most wretched woman from Borgo-Allegri. But come this way tomorrow afternoon about three o'clock

when I will await you on the doorstep and,
as a sign that it will be you, when you are
right in front of the door, blow your nose
in this handkerchief; ' (she here gave him
a handkerchief with a black silk border)
' yes, do that, and I promise you that I will
let you in.   You may then say to me what
you like, anything proper I mean ; do not
go and think the contrary.'

Having said this she shut the window in
his face without even shaking hands and;
running off to her mistress, told her what
had happened.   The lady raised her hands
to heaven and, considering the moment had
certainly come when her stratagem was going to succeed, thanked her with a thousand
kisses and caresses.

Meanwhile Carlo went home to bed, but
was unable to sleep a wink through thinking of what could be done to make the
Abbot give the sign.   He got up wholly
absorbed by this problem and repaired
about mass-time to Nunziata where, chanc-
ing to meet his friend Girolamo Firenzuola,
who was wont to spend the whole day with
the Abbot, he related his adventure of
the previous evening and craved his help
and advice regarding the sign to be given.

Firenzuola at once told him to be of good
hope and, if that was his only trouble, he
could be at peace for he himself would do
whatever was needed.   After these words
he took the handkerchief and left his friend.

When the time appeared to him suitable,
he went to the Abbot, took him for a walk
and, passing from one topic to another
while strolling along, he led him unsuspect-
ingly by Agnoletta's house.   When they
were right bang in front of the door, Firenzuola said to the Abbot, previously putting
the handkerchief into his hand: 'Wipe
your nose, old chap, it's all dirty.'   The
Abbot who thought no more about it, took
the handkerchief and blew into it, and Laldomine and Agnoletta firmly believed that
he had only blown his nose to give the
agreed-on sign, and they rejoiced accordingly.

The two young men said no more to each
other and they directed their steps towards
the San Giovanni Square ; there Firenzuola
asked the Abbot's permission to leave and
he went off to Carlo who was waiting for
him near the hospital of the Orphelines.
He told him exactly what had taken place,
then, bidding him goodbye, he left him

alone in his joy.

The night having come, Carlo went about nine o'clock to the house of the two women and, having planted himself beside the same window as before, awaited the coming of Laldomine.

He had not been there very long when the servant, prompted by her who was still more eager than Carlo, came to the window, saw him, recognized him as the visitor of yestereve, and nodded to him to go to the door. Carlo went to the door and, finding it open, entered the house quietly. He wanted, as soon as he was inside, to take Laldomine in his arms and kiss her, but she, being faithful to her mistress, would listen to nothing and bade him stay there very tranquilly until Madam had gone to bed. Then, feigning that somebody was calling her, she left the hall and went off to Agnoletta who was eagerly awaiting the issue of all this. When she found out that the Abbot was in her house, if she was not delighted at it, well—I ask you to read on.

Agnoletta had a bed made up with the finest clothes in a room next the hall, and then told Laldomine to go for the Abbot and make him sleep there. The maid

groped her way back to Carlo and silently
led him into the chamber, telling him to
take off his clothes and get into bed. She
then went out, pretending she was going to
see if her mistress was asleep and, before
much time had passed, Madonna Agnoletta
well bathed and perfumed, went softly to
him, instead and in place of Laldomine,
and got into bed beside him.

Although the darkness contrived to conceal her beauty, her dazzling whiteness was
such that it was hard for her to disguise
herself. In the belief the two lovers were
in, of being, the one with Laldomine and
the other with the Abbot, they were afraid
to converse, and it was by smacks, tight
embraces and all the endearments natural
to so lucky a couple that they understood
each other, making each other the tenderest
caresses as you may imagine. If any fond
ejaculation chanced to pass their lips, it
was murmured so low that the other could
not hear it, and, wondering at such discretion, they were only the gladder for it.
But what gives me most mind to laugh
when I think of it all, is the mutual satis-
faction they felt for having arrived at their
end by so amusing a drollery. While she

was laughing to herself for having so nicely taken him in, he was laughing at her for having been taken in, and they were both so pleased with this fine fun that it enhanced their enjoyment two-fold. Without in the least suspecting who one or the other was, they spent the whole night in such amusement, such rejoicings, and such transports that they could have wished it an eternity long.

When morning dawned Agnoletta got up and, pretending she was going I know not where, sent Laldomine in her place. She made Carlo dress himself quickly, and then let him out secretly by a back-door. But that this night which had been the first should not also be the last, they agreed that whenever Girolamo was away they would take advantage of the occasion, and so they often met, without anyone being the wiser.

Judge, lovely youths, whether this lady's craft was great; she knew, under another's name and without risking her honor, how to arrange for a pleasant journey through life's uncharted seas!

ROMANCE IV

PENANCE

You must know there lived in the Pisto-
jan mountains, a long time ago, a priest
named Dom Giovanni, curate of Santa
Maria of Quarantola ; and, in order to keep
up the usual custom of country priests, he
fell madly in love with one of his parishon-
iers. Her name was Tonia and she was the
wife of one of the local big guns, a man
named Giovanni, but better known as Ciarpaglia. This Tonia was perhaps twenty-
two ; she was well set up and bonny, and
rather dark owing to the excessive love the
sun bore her. Among other capacities,
such as being skilled in nailing down a base
coin and digging a straight furrow, she was
also the best dancer in the place, and if

anybody unfortunately chanced to go through the sets with her, after the riga-doon, she was so longwinded that she would put a hundred men out of breath. Happy indeed was he who could dance a single heat with her, and I can assure you that she had been the cause of more than one complaint. .

Now, when this jolly damsel discovered the clerical passion, not being in the least intimidated by it, she occasionally laid her-self out to cajole him, and he jumped with joy like a two-year-old. He was gnawing into her more and more every day and, without ever speaking of anything below the waist, he would come and chat with her for a couple of hours, telling her the fun-niest tales you ever heard. She, who was more cunning than the devil, in order to see if he was very accommodating with folks and if he held out stoutly against the temptation of the purse, always asked him for some little trifle whenever she knew he was going to town, such as two farthings' worth of Levant red, a little ceruse, a buckle for her belt, or some similar bauble. The priest used to spend his money on her as willingly as he would on a church repair.

With all this, he was waiting ; and, whether he was satisfied with dressing as a beau for show, by wearing the traditional garb of an angel, and that in Platonic love he found his needs supplied ; or whether he was afraid of the husband, or no matter why—he was waiting until she would say to him : 'Ser Giovanni, do come to bed with me.'

This lasted fully two months, which he spent in feeding on the wind, like the clown's donkey, while she made some little profit by him, but things got no forwarder. At length, whether Tonia took it too easy like a woman who was not ashamed to ask him repeatedly for a pair of yellow buskins, those in fashion, split at the sides and laced with a string, then a pair of perforated galoches with lovely white bridles set off with all sorts of arabesques, or whether it was the urge of Nature which daily waxed more urgent, or for no matter what other motive, he thought it would be well on the first occasion that should present itself and whatever might come of it, to ask her fair and square if there was anything doing.

One day when he espied her alone he brought her a salad from his garden, for he

had the finest cabbage lettuce ever you did
see, and, after having given it her, he went
and sat in front of her and ogled her withal.
He then burst into the following speech :
‘ Well ! look how pretty she is to-day, this
dear Tonia. By the Gospel, I know not
what I have not done for you. Oh ! you
are fairer than the women on that picture
of the temptation of Saint Anthony which
Frusino di Meo Puliti recently painted in
our church for the salvation of his soul.
What lady of Pistoja is as handsome as you ?
See if those two lips do not resemble the
border of my festival chasuble ! What joy
even to bite them, and the mark thereof to
remain till vintage-time ! Faith, I swear
to you by the Seven Virtues of the Mass, if
I were not a priest and you not married, I
should do what the occasion suggests. Oh,
the delicious feasts I should make of you !
The deuce take it if I should not get rid of
the rage which torments my belly ! ’

While our gentleman was thus holding
forth, Tonia remained as though half vexed,
with one eye threatening and the other in-
viting. When he had ended his fine har-
angue she, while shaking her head, replied :
‘ Ah ! monseignor, come, come ! you have

no .need to poke fun at me. If I do not please you, I do not mind so long as I please my husband.'

The priest, who already felt sure of the affair and shook with joy like a wagtail, took heart and continued : 'Happy if you pleased me much less, my jewel, for you compel me to follow you about. Oh ! what would I not give to be able to touch but once those rosebuds you have in your stays. They consume me quicker than a farthing candle before the altar ! ' Tonia replied : ' Now I wonder what you really would pay ? Why, you are more niggardly than a cock ! Faith, he who names a priest names a beggar, and perhaps you don't mean to spend even a copper ! As if I did not know you made a stepmother's face when I asked you the other day for those galoches ! Anybody might think I was asking you for the world and all. I know very well that when your neighbor Mencaglio wanted something from Tentennino's wife, he jolly well had to pay half the price of that petticoat she had made for All Saints' Day. And you know enough about petticoats to know that that wasn't bought for nothing.' ' By the body of Saint Nothingatall, my dear Tonia,'

cried the priest, ' you are a thousand times
wrong; for I am more open-handed with
women than anyone else I know, and I
never go to town without spending at least
two bolognini with the pretty ladies who
live behind the Prior's Palace. That being
so, think of what I would do for you with
your lovely figure ! You have so stirred up
my liver and tripes that I have no longer
any leisure to despatch a mouthful of the
Office and, to tell you the truth, I fear you
have ensorcelled me.'

Hearing such fine promises, the cunning
dame wished to make a trial of him and so
she told him that she would be happy to
give herself to him for his pleasure, provided that he would bind himself to buy her a
pair of wide yellow serge sleeves edged with
green velvet, also green ribbons which they
tie in the hair and let float about in the air,
a green hair-net with its ear-knot, and, besides, to lend her three bolognini for a piece
of linen from the weaver's ; if not, he had
only to return to his pretty ladies who serv-
ed him so well for his two bolognini.

The poor priest, whose clapper was quite
ready for the bell, unwilling to lose so fine
an opportunity, promised her not only the

sleeves, but the petticoat with an under
one as well, and he wanted straightway to
join battle, when she, seeming rather to
enjoy the flirting exclaimed : ' Oh, oh !
Dom Giovanni, my darling, just look and
see if you have not by chance a few odd
coppers in your pocket. I am very hard
up and, believe me, my old man hasn't a
rag of a shirt to put on his back.'

The good priest would have preferred to
have been granted credit, and he tried to
make out that he was a bit short, but that,
when the Complines were ended, he would
go straight to the church and look in the
candle boxes to see if there was enough in
them to make up the amount and, if so, he
would let her have the cash at once. But
Tonia, noticing how he was imposing on
her, pretended she was vexed and she said
to him in a sour tone of voice : ' Did I not
say that you are as mean as they make
'em ? Clear out ! By the Cross, you shall
not lay a hand on me till you have shelled
out. I'm taking a lesson out of the book
of you priests—you who will not sing unless
you get paid on the nail ! It suffices, I
think, if I am willing to wait for the rest
until you have been to town ; but a trifle

on account I must have, for I do not know
which way to turn for a penny.'

'Look here now, do not get angry, my
dear Toniotta; I will just see whether by
any possible chance I have some money on
me.' Thus speaking, he pulled out of his
breeches pocket a small purse full of holes
from which he laboriously squeezed a few
coppers which, with many a wry grimace,
he paid over one by one. No sooner was it
done than she, all merry, led him away to
a nearby barn to help him chime his bells
a bit. And there they met more than once
until such time as he went to Pistoja.

When he was on his return, whether it
was that he had lost his memory or was
grieved to spend his money, he at any rate
only bought· the net, which he took her,
and apologized because he had forgotten
the sleeves at home. He promised to bring
them next day and he knew so well how to
wheedle her that, taking the net, she was
still pleased to chime the triple bob-major.
But one day and another passed and the
mean old scamp brought neither sleeves
nor cuffs. Tonia began to be vexed and
one fine evening let fly at him with a few
complimentary remarks. He who had

pretty fairly shaken his donkey's bridle,
thinking that if she wanted sleeves she had
only to buy them, replied to her so briskly
that she was highly displeased with him
and resolved to avenge herself 'Away,
away, you petticoated swindler,' said she
to herself, while reproaching herself for her
folly; 'if I don't make you sit up for it,
may a fever burn me up! I have been
silly to entangle myself with so despicable
a brood, as if I had not heard it said a
thousand times that they are all of the
same savor; but let it rest there for now.'

The better to show what her anger was,
she remained three or four days without
even looking at him, then, in order to be
the more easily able to avenge herself on
him according to the scheme she had conceived, she began again to coax him with
provoking words and, without speaking
about the sleeves, pretended she had made
peace with him.

One day, when the moment seemed propitious for the execution of her plan, she
called him to her and told him how her
Ciarpaglia had gone to Cutigliano and begged him, if he wished to treat himself to an
agreeable pleasure with her, to come to the

house for her about None-time, when she
would be alone and expecting him; that if
by chance he did not find her in, to kindly
wait a bit as she would soon be back.

Ask not whether Dom Caprone felt happy at such a request; he stood in his slip-
pers, saying to himself: ' I must say I was
surprised at her being so long about
falling in love with me. You can see the
sleeves haven't bothered her much. I was
a fool to give her anything at all; it would
have been all the same by now. I'll tell
you what, Dom Giovanni, if you don't get
more than your money's worth now, I shall
think you're the biggest fool ever.'

While thus talking to himself, he was
awaiting the appointed hour, and it had no
sooner come than he did as the woman had
bidden him. The minx had that morning
related to her husband how the priest had
more than once requested her for her virtue, and the present arrangement was
agreed on by them in order to inflict a severe chastisement on the priest.

As soon as the woman perceived Dom
Giovanni entering, she beckoned to Ciarpaglia and one of his brothers who were
watching out for this moment, and, preced-

ing them softly, went off for the gallant
who was already on the bed with his feet in
the air. Dom Giovanni had no sooner espied her than, without doubting anything,
he went to meet her. Saluting her politely,
he tried to throw his arms round her neck
and kiss her in the French fashion; but he
had hardly time to accost her when Ciarpaglia appeared, crying like a madman : ' Ah !
you whoremonger of a priest—you shaven
pate ! Wait, wait till I drop on you ! Is
that the way a pious priest behaves, eh ?
May God heap calamities on you, you beggar's get ! Go and herd swine ! Be off to
the sty, and not to the church, you hypo-
crite ! ' Then turning aside to the brother,
in a rage that had no equal, he continued :
' Don't hold me back—let me get at him—
or I will do you an injury. Leave it to me !
I'll blood my wife, and eat this traitor's
heart, red hot, red hot ! '

While the man was thus raving, the
priest, breech-befouled, had slunk in a funk
beneath the bed, and yelled for mercy with
all his might. But it was so much chaff
thrown against the wind, because Ciarpaglia
was fully determined that for once it should
be the layman who would impose penance

on the priest. He had is this very room a
large chest which had lain there since the
time of his great grandfather, and in which
his wife kept the best of her clothes. He
opened it, flung out all the gewgaws and,
dragging the priest from under the bed,
made him pull his breeches down, which
the latter had, while waiting for Tonia, already unlaced, not to let her languish too
long, as I guess ; he seized his testicles,
which the priest had stout and of fair length
as befitted a gallant, put them into the
chest, nailed down the lid, then with a big
key stuffed up the keyhole and, having got
his brother to give him an old notched razor, he laid this on the chest without a
word of explanation and then went off to
his work.

The unfortunate priest, thus left in the
state you may imagine, felt such pain at
first that he was like to faint. Fortunately
the lock was so dislocated that the bolt
scarcely entered the hasp, and there was a
gap between the lid and the box, so at first
our hero came to no great harm. Nevertheless, every time he caught sight of the
razor and thought of the place where he
had been seized, such agony pressed on his

heart that he wondered he was not yet
dead; had he not forced himself to keep
at his ease awhile in saying to himself that
they only wanted to frighten him, and that
they would not be long before coming to
free him from this torture, I believe he
would have been really dead.

After he had remained pretty long unde-
cided between doubt and hope, seeing nobody was coming to his aid, and his flesh in
beginning to swell was causing him considerable pain, he started to cry for help. No
help came; he then attempted to break the
lock. The only result was to tire himself
and increase the pain in the tumefying flesh.
He then ceased from exciting himself and
began to implore assistance.

Assistance did not come, mercy was ab-
sent, and the pain got worse and worse.
Despairing of getting safely out of the affair, he took hold of the razor in the firm
resolution to end such agony, even at the
cost of his life; but straightway seized
with a cowardly weakness and compassion
for himself, he cried out while weeping:
'Oh my God! what have I done to deserve
this? Cursed be Tonia and the first day I
ever set eyes on her!' Then oppressed by

an inexpressible torment, he became silent.

Some time after, he fixed his eyes on the razor, took hold of it again and, slightly grazing the skin, tried how it hurt him; but he had hardly drawn it nigh when there came over him such a cold sweat, a dread, a swoon, that he felt himself fainting off. No longer knowing what to do, worn out by fatigue, he lay on his belly across the chest, and while now whining, now sighing, now yelling, now offering himself to God, now blaspheming, the pain exasperated him and became so acute that, being no longer able to bear it, he saw himself forced to use the only means which remained to him for his deliverance. Making a virtue of necessity, he grasped the razor, exercised on himself the vengeance of Ciarpaglia and separated himself from his privy parts. The operation caused him so terrible a pain that he dropped down half dead, and bellowing like a wounded bull. The folks that Ciarpaglia had carefully gathered came running at this noise, and they tended the priest so that he escaped with his life—if it can be called living to be deprived of the mainstay of life.

ROMANCE V

TEMPTATION OF THE FLESH

There was at Perugia, and still is to-day,
a very rich convent crowded with Perugian
ladies who, for want of knowing my excellent receipt, had erred from their father,
Saint Benedict's, rule.

Most of the nuns, perhaps all, being thoroughly in accord with the abbess, occupied
themselves only in procuring those pleasures of which the want of a dowry, the pa-
pas' avarice, the mammas' preferences, the
stepmothers' jealousy or other similar accidents had deprived them, and they had
carried them to such a pitch that one might
easily find virtue everywhere, save in this
holy retreat. The bishop was therefore
obliged, far more by the complaints which

the folks of the place had frequently made him than by any vigilance or solicitude on his part, to find some remedy against their disorderly life. He therefore ordered part of them, chiefly those who, grown old in wickedness, were but little fit to enter on a new life, to be sent away. He kept the rest and added to them a certain number of girls, as well as those chosen in other convents of purer morals. Among the latter was a venerable matron who had lived for more than forty years in the convent of Monte Lucci in an odor of sanctity, and he appointed her as abbess. By means of new rules and a good example she at length brought the house to a suitable observance.

This abbess had ordered among other prescriptions that, between None and Vespers, at the chiming of a hundred bells which she took the greatest care to have rung, all the nuns should be bound to betake themselves to the chapel, or their cells, or wherever they would like best, and to remain there one half-hour in prayer, to beseech the good Lord to remove from them all evil temptations which might come from the flesh; the one she saw putting most fervor in this practice, her she considered to be of better will in living well than any other, believing, and she was not mistaken, that the sting of the flesh once mastered, all the rest would be easy. But, for the reason that what is the outcome of violence does not last long, and pestilent water easily spreads again over its former bed, it turned out that among the old ones who had remained, a certain Sister Appellagia, both young and pretty, could no longer endure to have, in order to satisfy her already corrupted appetite, but prayers and the sound of bells. Previous to the reforms she had fallen in love with a young man of Perugia who was noble and very rich, and who enjoyed great favor with Giovan-Paolo Baglione ; he too loved her exceedingly, and they had so well known how to act that they were often together in the nun's cell for three or four hours at a time, and jolly hours and all ! This was done so secretly that it was impossible for anyone to notice it but, as she could not, for fear of giving the alarm, remain locked up with him all day long in her room as she would have wished, and besides she was obliged to keep with the other sisters in the convent for the usual exercises of the house, as soon

as she heard the blessed bell she ran quickly to her cell, under pretext of the said
prayer, so quickly that she seemed going
up to paradise.   The abbess, who had never suspected anything, seeing her so exact
in this intention, had conceived the highest
opinion of her.

Now it so happened one day that one of
the ancient nuns having gone into the garden to gather a little salad to be sent to
some relation, heard the temptation-bell
ring, and she, fearing the messenger might
go away without the salad, decided to go
on filling her basket and to let the prayer
slide.   Tidings of this misdeed were immediately carried to the abbess who, having
called the delinquent to her, made a row
about it, whato, great God !   Among other
things she said to her, and what stung her
most was, that she should take as a model
Sister Appellagia, who never found herself
so busy in anything of no matter how much
importance, but she very quickly left it the
moment she heard that bell ringing.

When the nun, who was perhaps better
acquainted with the young brood of the
convent than the abbess, saw herself re-
proached by the example of Sister Appell-

agia, she would listen no further and all in
a rage she said to herself : 'To be sure, I
must indeed see whence come so much fervor and devotion. There is something fishy
at the bottom of it, oh! yes, and I shall
just go and find out what she does in her
cell. Only let to-morrow come, and I'll
make the whole convent laugh.' While
speaking to herself in this way, and preg-
nant with an evil will, she waited till the
next day for the temptation-bell to ring ;
the moment having come, the cussed nun,
as soon as she saw Sister Appellagia running to her cell in order to flee the temptation, softly drew near the door, made a hole
in a certain opening which was covered inside with a sheet of paper, and discovered
how the learned young damsel had found
the true means of freeing herself from temptation. Without making the slightest noise
she went off full of glee to the abbess, told
her how things stood, and took her to see
the game of backgammon. I could never
describe to you the intense pain and trouble
which the poor abbess felt on hearing so
hideous a story, for it seemed to her indeed
that she had lost her time and pains in effecting so many reforms. Fired with rage,

she went to Appellagia's cell, burst open
the door and, beholding with her very eyes
what she had probably never even dreamt
of before, she nearly collapsed with grief.
Turning to the little nun, she called her the
grossest names that were ever addressed to
a woman of this kind taken in a similar
case. 'This was then, you devil's get, the
motive of your devotion ! It is for this you
showed yourself so prompt in running to
lock yourself in your cell, you nasty, bare-
faced baggage ! So the teachings inculcat-
ed on you, the warnings given you, and the
new reforms have all produced this fine
fruit ! Is it for this I left Monte Lucci, to
be witness of such ignominy, to behold with
my own eyes within the space of two
months what I had not even imagined in
thought in forty years ! God grant that I
stay no longer here, where the Devil has so
much power and audacity ! '

Having addressed these words and many
more to the young girl, she turned to upbraid the man and warn him what his end
would be if he did not quickly turn from
his evil ways. Returning then to the sister, she added : 'For this one, the proflig-
ate, I shall inflict such a chastisement as

will fit so enormous a crime.' But Appellagia, who was beginning to grow tired of
these reproaches, could bear them no longer and, displaying a countenance which
would have made one say : " She indeed is
beautiful and good," spoke in this manner :
' Madam, you make much ado about nothing, and in my opinion you are a thousand times wrong. Tell me, prithee, why
have you prescribed that every day at the
sound of the bell we offer up a private oris-
on, if it be not that every one of us be delivered from the temptation of the flesh ?
What better means could you invent than
the one I have discovered myself ? What
other road could we take that would give
such rest and peace ? The prayers and acts
of your invention only strengthen our temptations, whereas by my method I can get
to sleep with my mind as free from naughty
fancies as I sincerely hope yours is. Anyhow, to cut a long story short, either allow
me to preserve myself from temptation as
I understand things, or give me leave to go
where I think fit ; for my part I do not in-
tend to trouble the ears of the Lord by day,
only to find myself tempted and tormented
all through the night.'

The abbess, on hearing her give so impudent an answer, considered that it would be better policy and more profitable to the convent to pack her off than to keep her against her will. The young man also begged for the nun's release, and this decided the abbess. She at once gave the nun permission to quit the convent, and the quicker the better. And on that very same night the little strumpet went off to sleep at the young man's house, and she delivered herself from the temptation of the flesh during many long months, nor did she need to await the warning sound of a bell.

ROMANCE VI

THE TWO FRIENDS

Many years ago there lived at Florence
two young men of high descent and great
wealth, the one named Lapo Tornaquinci,
the other Niccolo of the Albizi, who had,
from their earliest boyhood, contracted so
close a friendship, that one would have fancied they could only live together.

They had been living thus for ten years,
when Niccolo's father departed this life,
leaving his son more than thirty thousand
ducats' worth of goods, and, as Lapo was
in need of a hundred ducats, Niccolo not
only obliged him with the amount without
even waiting to be asked for it, but begged
him to consider himself a part-owner of the
fortune : tokens indeed of a truly noble and

virtuous soul, worthy of causing the highest
hopes to be conceived, had not the too
emancipated youthfulness, naturally prone
to evil, the wealth acquired without work,
and the somewhat unpraiseworthy frequent-
ings, engaged him in a wicked life. Indeed,
as he followed the example of those who at
night go to bed poor and rise in the morning rich, after having long drudged in misery, he soon had round him a gang of fellows of so depraved a life, that they would
have removed the aureola from the greatest
saint's head ; and those keeping company
with him, now at dinner, now at supper,
taking him to such and such a feast or to
the house of some lost woman, made him
squander so much money that it really was
shameful. His friend, being a very sober
and reserved young man, on seeing this,
was grieved to the bottom of his heart and
was all day long behind him to recall him
to righteousness, to rebuke him for his
wrongs, and to render him all the kind acts
which their friendship demanded. But all
was in vain. The new cronies had, with
their dishonorable pastimes and pernicious
counsels, more sway over him than Lapo
with his wise warnings ; and these fellows,

who were watching Lapo, related so much
evil to Niccolo about him and cried him
down to such a degree that, having begun
by detaching himself from him, he ended
by fleeing from him, thus intimating that
he intended to live in his own way. Lapo,
when once sure of the fact, ceased through
weariness from being always after him, and,
unable to do anything for him, let him conduct himself as he pleased. The upshot
was that the poor fool, continuing to live
as he ought not to do, saw an event befall
him of which he was but little thinking.

Just at that time there was at Florence
a handsome and graceful young widow of
pleasing manners who, having contracted
the habit, even during the lifetime of her
husband, of preferring money to honor,
without casting a further thought cn the
family in which she was born or that into
which she had entered by marriage, the
both being of great nobility, she easily
gratified young men with her love, provided
they were not only fine fellows in appearance but were flush of money and generous.

Both before and during her widowhood
she had plucked more than one pigeon
clean, though passing for a second Saint

Bridget in the eyes of her relatives.

At the first tidings she had of Niccolo's fortune and the pace he was going, she at once founded great projects on him and, having secured an introduction, began to pretend she was smitten by him. Then, as though she could no longer conceal her infatuation, she set to entice him night and day with letters and messengers. I have no need to tell you whether Niccolo, who had been persuaded by his cronies that he was a fair devil with the ladies, was pleased with himself or not. Happy was he who could stick in his little word to flatter him, to congratulate him on his latest conquest and extol the lady to the skies! More than one dinner was wheedled out of him over this affair, and they wound him up so well than nothing else would suit any longer but discussing the lady's charms with these precious rascals. And she knew how to get round him so nicely that, while pretending she was dying of love, she succeeded in finding herself alone with him to do what she had already done with many others.

Being pretty, and having a way with her, she knew how to make a man dote on her better than any strut who had spent twen-

ty years on her greens, sometimes using the
mildest expressions in the world, sometimes
the harshest, to-day feigning she is unable
to live any longer without him, so much
she loved him, and to-morrow making him
jealous with a new sweetheart, warning him
that the moment was come to wed her,
then wishing it no longer, banging her door
in his face, again running after him, at another time pretending to be big with child,
she so exasperated the poor wretch that he
completely lost his bearings. All things
else had gone out of his head, his affairs remained at random, the new friends as well
as the old were thrown aside; diversions,
games, suppers were all, all for her, when
she wished and as she wished them. From
the moment she perceived that the bird
had no further need of being tamed, she set
her mind on clipping his wings so that he
could not fly away, and she succeeded in it
pretty well, not only to estrange Lapo who
was his true friend, but to create mischief
in the hearts of his other friends of jovial
time who had themselves thrown him into
her clutches. And it seemed to them that
all that the pretty lady racked out of Niccolo came from their purses, and they were

quite right, for the strut finally reduced
him by her craft and intrigues to such an
extremity that, far from being able to give
them a dinner or supper, he had not enough
money left to feed himself.

When he saw to what state he was come,
he recognized how much better he would
have done by lending an ear to the advice
of Lapo than listening to the flatteries of
his new favorites, and he realised besides
what a wretched end the love of these women always has, who offer the pleasures of
their bodies to the first comer, not indeed
through tender affection, but for greed of
gain. Lucrezia (I now remember this lady's name), seeing the crown pieces were
beginning to be missing with him and that
he would soon run out, had nevertheless
known how to carry her mock love to the
end ; she then began to assume such manners with him that he could very well perceive how dimly her fire was blazing. But
what pained him most was the discovery of
a new amorous caprice in his mistress. She
had recently learnt that a certain Simone
Davizi had, by his father's death, become
very wealthy, and she fell in love with him
at once and to such a degree that she com-

pletely forgot Niccolo. A wise, prudent and fortunate young woman, truly! She knew so well how to read one's eyes and instruct one's heart, that she discovered beauty among men in proportion as she saw they had gold or silver, and she felt most love when she heard the coins jingle.

Niccolo clearly saw that his affairs were going from bad to worse, and that he was being treated ignominiously by her whom he had cherished more than his life; but, far from decreasing in ratio to these outrages, his love, or more properly his rage, increased day by day. He longed to be with her as in the past and, finding no chance for it, he thundered against himself and her. He knew not on what to set his mind and his state inspired pity. The pals of his gay time had come with his fortune, and with it they had vanished. His rela-'tions would see him no more, his neighbors laughed at him, and strangers used to mock him.

Having well and duly considered all this on several occasions, he fell into such despair that he deliberated, as a last resource, on putting an end by some horrible death to such suffering, and perhaps he would

have put his idea into execution had he not,
while recalling to mind the close friendship
which had united him to Lapo and considering it as a sure thing that the latter would
not have lost the remembrance of so tender
an affection, thought it well on his part to
go and see him, leaving aside all false shame,
to relate to him his mishap and to beg his
pardon, for God's sake. He therefore went
to him without more ado, and did what he
had resolved on.

Lapo who had, as they say, let three
loaves pass for a couple, being unable to
prevent it, did not fail to take pity on Niccolo, seeing him according to his own ac-
knowledgements plunged into a completer
ruin than he would have supposed ; he was
greatly afflicted at it and knowing that his
friend was in more need of help then counsel, said kindly to him : ' Niccolo, I do not
wish to act like those who, after having
warned their friend to no purpose, reproach
him with not having listened to their advice ; those, I think, seek only to glorify
themselves in blaming whoever has not lent
an ear to their warnings. You are aware
that, when I saw you entering into that
way which led you to where I would rather

you were not, I fulfilled with my words the
duty of a friend.   Now that you are arrived
at the end, it is not words which any longer suffice, and I mean not to fail by my
acts in the same duty.   I shall act as if I
had sinned with you, and with you I shall
undergo penance, sweet penance indeed,
since it will give me the opportunity of
showing what my heart is to my friend.
The duty I wish to fulfil is as laudable and
worthy of recommendation as it has always
been, but very few men have discharged it,
and this is the clearest proof of its merit ; I
too desire to be reckoned among this small
number and, leaving words aside, wish to
show you the effects.   Come therefore with
me.'   Without another word he took him
into his room and, having opened his mon-
ey-box, gave him such a sum, that Niccolo
might judge how much he loved him.   He
then exhorted him by kind words to be of
good cheer and made him understand that,
when this money was spent, he would not
fail to supply him with more, as much and
as often as he wanted.   After having made
him so generous a present and given such
bright hopes for the future, Lapo began in
a most friendly tone to criticize his past

life, to censure his connexion with that woman; and these words had such influence
over Niccolo that, if they did not dislodge
her at once from his thoughts, they nevertheless infused into his heart a certain regret for what he had done and excited a
certain shame in him. He still loved the
woman, and still longed for an occasion to
slake his passion. But the treacherous fe-
male was not long before finding out that
he was in funds again; conjecturing that
everything had turned out to her greater
advantage and not wishing to let him slip
from her, she began a second time to importune him with letters, and so frequently
withal that Niccolo was obliged to let himself be locked again in her arms. She persuaded him that he was finer than ever;
that she more than ever wished him well;
that all which had sprung up between them
was no fault of hers, but of some relation
or maid; that the very great love he bore
her, that love which often causes the surest
eye to see awry, had made him jealous
about a thing which was far from being
true; and she knew so nicely how to fool
the poor devil that she squeezed many
crown pieces out of him. And she would

have had all his money had it not haply
come to pass, as his cruel destiny would
have it, that, one night among others while
he was with her and had fallen asleep from
fatigue after their amorous pleasures, she,
who was not asleep, heard by certain understood signs her new lover passing by
outside. Allured by her evil genius, she
persuaded herself that Niccolo had, as they
say, tied the ass to the right peg, and she
longed to go as far as the door to amuse
herself awhile with the other. She got up,
threw a light covering over her shoulders,
went down very quietly to the backdoor
and invited her lover in. One word leads
to another; from words to deeds is easy
going; they deemed themselves in such se-
curity owing to the deep sleep of Niccolo
that they remained thus far longer than
was needed. Niccolo woke up just in the
middle of the affair and, not finding Lucrezia beside him, was greatly surprised. He
called her several times and, getting no answer, guessed the truth. He immediately
jumped to his feet, dressed himself as best
he could while groping in the dark, and,
having stuck a sword in his belt, crept silently up to them. Before either of the

guilty pair noticed anything he was at their
pillow and, beholding them stretched on
sacks of flour, he was all of a sudden carried
off with such wrath, such madness, that,
without reflecting on what he was doing, he
drew his sword and dealt both of them at
once such a well-directed cut that he almost
lopped off Simone's head, while grievously
wounding the woman's arm ; then, his ire
only increasing, he redoubled the cuts and
only stopped when he saw that they both
lay dead. All the inmates came running
at this hubbub, they began to bewail the
amiable young woman and each one had
his word to stick in ; as to Niccolo, as if he
made no question about the crime he had
committed, he walked out of the house,
satisfied that he had performed a great feat.
Being still mad with fury and still grasping
his reeking sword, he was running to Lapo's
house, quite delighted to go and have a
laugh over so fine an exploit, when he just
fell into a squadron of the Bargello who,
seeing him running in such a manner, sur-
mised he was guilty of some crime and so
dragged him off to jail. There, without
there being need of pressing or torturing
him, he confessed how the thing had hap-

pened and, found guilty of manslaughter,
was sentenced to death. But his generous
friend deemed that this was the moment to
show what the greatness, the strength, of
friendship may be : he did so much with
the aid of friends and money that he saved
his life for him. The sentence was com-
muted to banishment for life to Barletta,
in Apulia. That did not satisfy Lapo ; he
condemned himself to exile and, forsaking
his sweet and pleasing country, went to live
with Niccolo, in a wretched land where he
supplied his wants out of his private fortune. He brought back the wandering
mind of his friend to the study of literature
and other worthy occupations, and they
both gained the esteem of the king of the
country. He, in the course of time, obtained leave for Niccolo to live at Naples, and
there the two friends lived till Niccolo's
death, when Lapo had him taken to Flor-
and buried him among his kindred. He
likewise ordered that after his own death he
was to be buried in the same grave, so that
in death, as in life, they should not be
divided.

ROMANCE VII

THE SEWED-UP BRIDE

There still lived in Florence, not many
months ago, a certain Zanobi di Piero del
Cima, one of those good Christians who re-
commend themselves to the Crucifix of San
Giovanni, Chiarito or San Pier del Murrone;
he had somewhat more confidence in the
Annunciation of San Marco than in that of
the Servites, and he used to say it was old-
er and quainter. He gave other reasons
for his preference, such as the angel's profile
was sharper, the dove was whiter, and other like motives. I know he let himself be
carried off more than once to severely upbraid the prior because he did not keep it
veiled, stating that nothing had given so
great a reputation to that of the Servites

and the Cintola of Prato, as the showing of
them with much ado and many ceremonies.
With all that, he was a fine fellow ; he oft-
en went to confession, fasted every Friday,
assisted at Complines on all festival days
and, when he made vows to these Crucifixes,
he observed them as scrupulously as grocers
weigh pepper, even though it clearly cost
him money, for in all he spent on them at
least a third of his income.   In this way,
without wife or children, he lived an easy
and comfortable life with an old woman
who was in his house for forty years.

Now this good old man was desirous of
cutting a figure among the consuls of his
Art, and he made a vow to the Crucifixes
which were in the Oratory of the Servites
that if he obtained this dignity he would
give a hundred pounds in silver to some
lass as a dowry.   His vow was heard, and
this was surely a great miracle for the Crucifixes had not even yet been painted !

The simpleton had no sooner heard the
news of his election than, quite overwhelm-
ed with joy and eager for compliments, he
gave an account of his vow to his confessor,
a certain Ser Giulano Bindi, rector of San
Remo, and a reputed saint.   The priest

mentioned to him a certain Monna Mechera da Calenzano of whom folks had whispered I know not what, implicating the priest himself; but I should affirm nothing about it on that account, for it is a sin to think evil of monks, and especially of those who hear confessions, who say mass with downcast eyes, and who have the care of souls, as well as the affairs of widows. Suffice it to say that he bore her affection and that, every time she came to Florence, she used to stay at his house. He informed her of what was in the air, and she set off at once in search of Zanobi and entreated him for God's sake to give the money to a daughter of hers who was ripe for marriage but penniless. Thanks to the cleric's assistance and her own clever coaxings, the silly fellow gave her a written promise, stating therein that as soon as a marriage was settled he would hand over a hundred pounds in hard cash. It has been asserted that he gave the woman no document, but simply promised by word of mouth, and that he gave the husband the writing later on; this is more likely, and agrees better with what you are going to see. Be the truth then as it may, and let each understand it as he will—I want no one's reproaches.

The gay old woman, once in possession of the promise, returned home quite merry and set herself to marry off her daughter. By the aid of her devoted priest she found a suitable husband ; but he, as soon as they had shaken hands, whether he had as a pledge the written engagement of Zanobi, or whether he received it from the mother-in-law, having given his word and the ring, was obliged to set out and spend a few weeks at Chianti on business, and he left with the intention of celebrating the wedding on his return.

It turned out that he was detained much longer than he had thought, so much so that Monna Mechera, believing he would not come back, was tempted to do a very funny thing and to even get hold of the hundred pounds. How she worked her daughter up to it and what her own end could really be, I cannot easily imagine ; suffice it to say she cast her eyes upon her neighbor, a certain big booby about twenty five years of age. Although this fellow acted the gawk he was a bit of a rake on the quiet. His name was Menicuccio dalle Prata.

One day the woman took him aside and said : 'Menicuccio, whenever you wish to do me a great favor, without its costing you anything, without your running any risk, you will be the means of my getting a hundred pounds as easily as picking them up in the street, and at the same time you will save my Sabatina from going to the bad. And here's how ! A Florentine has promised me that when my daughter gets married he will give her a hundred pounds as a dowry and, as you are aware, I have betrothed her to Giannella del Mangano who has since gone to the end of the earth and who has sent word that he will not return to get married unless I first send him the money. But the donor will not part with the cash until the girl is married, so I do not know what course to take, and meanwhile Sabatina suffers. To tell you the truth I am heartily sick of it, and for some time now I have felt uneasy, seeing all day messing round here certain men I would not like to trust. You know what it is if a girl is pretty and there is no man in the house ; folks respect nothing, so much the worse for the poor. I should like you to assist me in getting hold of this money, and

it would be easy if you will give your mind
to it. First, I will make you a present of a
beautiful brand-new shirt with quilted wrist
bands and embroidered collar, the finest to
be seen in the district; then I shall also
give you the money to buy yourself a new
pair of shoes and a cap.'

Imagine whether Menicuccio cocked his
ears at such fine offers; he replied to Monna Mechera : ' Faith, if this thing is possible, I am coming in on the ground-floor !
Anything, so long as I don't get pinched.'
' Eh, fool ! ' replied Monna Mechera, ' what
do you say ? Do you think I would let
you run the slightest risk ? God forbid !
Do you know what I want ? I want you
to pretend you are my daughter's husband.'

' Oh ! you want me to pose as your son-
in-law ? But everybody knows who he is.'

' Yes, here, but not at Florence. The
three of us will go there, you calling yourself Giannella, and you will tell this Florentine that you wish to get married at once.
As he has never seen you before, he will
believe you are the bridegroom and will
count you out the money. You will then
hand it over to me, and I shall thus be able
to compel Giannella to keep his promise.

Otherwise, I can see the job hanging on a twelve-month.'

The thing seemed easy enough to Menicuccio, were it not that he feared the Florentine might know him ; but the woman understood so well how to get round him that he finally agreed and said : ' All right, carry on ! I've had harder jobs, anyhow. But look here, you will have to pay me a carlino a day while the farce lasts, to make up for the time I lose from work.'

Agreeing, the woman took him home, and they talked the matter over with the girl, and arranged their plans.   Early next morning they set out for Florence.

Some people pretend that the young lass, who was all there, seeing in Menicuccio a big blond blockhead, a fellow fit to make one languish and safe as a eunuch, conceived the idea of enjoying herself.   Others say that he cared far more about the girl than he did about Monna Mechera's promises ; that, while showing himself a jovial clown, he was, as we say, a thorough blackguard who had played many dirty tricks.   However, I affirm nothing, though I rather fancy he was a bit of both.

They went off therefore, as I was saying,

in search of Zanobi, who was just walking
out from Laud in Or San Michele, and they
told him how they were coming for the hundred pounds, because the husband, Menicuccio, so they stated, wished to lead the
bride to the altar next Tuesday (it being
now Saturday), and that their intention
was to buy a bed at the Monday market,
and so on, and so forth.

The old man had arrived back the previous evening from Riboja where he had
been visiting a small demesne which he intended to purchase ; he received them most
kindly and told them he was wholly at their
disposal, but that he wanted to see the girl
married with his own eyes, and suffered
himself nowise to be played with.   Conse-
quently it would be his pleasure to have
them to supper, and to lend them a bed
and dispose of everything that would be re-
quisite, in order that the marriage might be
consummated in his house on the following
night.   Of course they agreed.

They went next morning, which was Sunday, to the wedding mass as man and wife,
and in the evening they supped at Zanobi's
table and abandoned themselves to all the
gaiety and diversion usual in like cases be-

tween newly married couples, to the great
joy of Zanobi who congratulated himself
on having been the means of such a charming union, and who hoped that his deed
would bring him further good luck.

When they all had supped their fill, and
bedtime had arrived, he made the young
couple understand that they were to go and
sleep in a room halfway up the house where
he usually slept his farmer whenever he
came to bring him a basket of apples.   He
told Monna Mechera that she would sleep
with his old servant, but she wanted to be
in the same room as her daughter.   He explained to her how unlawful this was, and
would on no account tolerate it.   She held
her peace, not wishing to create any sus-
picion in his mind, but she called Sabatina
to her and, having taken her aside, preach-
ed her a long sermon face to face, that she
should take precious good care not to let
Menicuccio sow his beans in the drills of
Monte Ficale.   Not contented with what
the cunning wench had promised and sworn
to her twenty times over, she sewed her up
in her chemise from head to foot with a
double thread so that it was impossible for
her to get out.   She next called Menicuccio

and, having made him swear that he would conduct himself as with his own sister, she put the couple to bed and then went off to her own room.

The bridegroom and bride had not been more than half an hour in bed when, whether it was the warmth of the blankets, or the itching of a little scab which Sabatina felt tickling her between her thighs, or whether she wished to micturate, or no matter why, she set about looking for the means of ripping the chemise, and she struggled so hard with her hands and feet that she worked herself entirely out of it. The poor boy, whose conscience was perhaps pricking him for being in such a place, began by stretching his legs and throwing out his arms as one does on waking; then, perceiving the change, as by mere chance, he laid his hands on the girl. She was undoubtedly a bad bedfellow, for she set to tumbling over his side; he did as much, and they were soon in each others arms. Menicuccio, being the stronger, rolled over on top and stormed the imminent breach; then thinking he had perhaps done wrong and wishing to make peace, he began to kiss and embrace her, but, as she seemed cross with him, he char-

ged to the assault once more. Eight times
did he renew the charge, till Sabatina, taking the offensive, dragged him underneath
herself and squeezed him so tightly that he
had to cry out. She too had matter for
whining, and began to weep; nevertheless,
she had done battle so boldly that I can
not think it was her first engagement.

At length the hour for rising came, and
when Monna Mechera saw that the chemise
was ripped, that the outlaws had violated
their ban and passed through Hollow Street
butchery, she felt like kicking up a row;
then, inspired with a better thought, in order not to disclose the plot, and knowing
besides that she had found what she was
looking for, held her peace as best she could
and, turning to Menicuccio, besought him
for God's sake not to say a word to a soul.
Without further parley, as soon as dressed,
they went off to Zanobi who was waiting
for them by the kitchen fire, where he was
explaining what the Flower of Virtue meant
to his old servant. The gay old dog wished them 'good morning' and 'many happy
returns,' gave them a good breakfast, then
handed them the money done up in a handkerchief. He next gave them his blessing,

begging them to visit him from time to time, then packed them off home, letting them take the written engagement with them.

They returned all merry and bright to Calenzano and, to compensate Menicuccio, the old woman allowed him to interview her daughter; for, since he had had his hands in the paste, she fancied that one does not soil the trough more to make ten loaves than one.

This state of things lasted perhaps two months, until Giannella the true husband came back. Shortly after his return he resolved to conclude the marriage and, without consulting the ma-in-law, which was the cause of all the wrangling, betook himself to Florence. He met Zanobi who was just hearing mass at the altar of the Virgin in Santa Maria del Campo and, after many twists and turns, asked him for the hundred pounds.

At this request, without answering a word, Zanobi burst out laughing, thinking that this was a joke, but Giannella began to bawl out that honest men do not give their word to deny it afterwards and that, if his money was not counted out to him,

he well knew where to go and see justice
done him, so that Zanobi, deviating for
once from his habits, was forced into a fury
and replied by a stream of insults, like any
other man. ' You rascal, you robber, where
do you think you are ? In the street, perhaps ? Three months ago Monna Mechera,
Sabatina, and her husband came to see me
and, in my house, under my very nose, consummated the marriage with all the usual
ceremonies. I handed them the money
myself, and now this thief comes and asks
for it again. It is true I forgot to get back
my agreement, I gave it no thought, not
suspecting that anyone would attempt such
a trick. This man must have stolen it from
them ; fortunately for me I entered it in
my book, I took note of everything, and
you cannot catch me, wretch. If you do
not get out of my sight I shall lodge a complaint and have you treated as you deserve.'
On seeing his bad humor, Giannella went
straight to the Episcopal Palace and had
him summoned. Zanobi presented himself,
related to the vicar how the thing had tak-
en place, and the vicar ordered Monna Mechera, her daughter, and Menicuccio to appear ; through them we learned all, even to

the story of the chemise, and how Sabatina won the final round. The vicar's sentence was, that the old hag should be flogged, that Menicuccio should give Giannella forty pounds which had been spent, and that Giannella should take Sabatina to his own home, asking no questions about her doings with Menicuccio. This latter, in order to find the forty pounds, was obliged to sell his land. They say the vicar gave this judgment because he had faked the marriage mass, but I do not think so. He had really married them and it is wrong to suggest otherwise. He proved what *Futuro caret* means, an adage which signifies that the fruit or rather the first-crop cost poor Menicuccio dearly. But he who possesses once for all does not always suffer !

ROMANCE VIII

The Precious Jewel

Should anybody say : 'They have just caught a fox,' you would not cry out a miracle, remembering the proverb : 'Foxes also allow themselves to be taken ,' you would be more inclined to think that the dexterity of some man or the courage of some animal had put the beast in this fix. But if you learned that a gentle dove, the first day she left the nest, had succeeded in taking two foxes, one of which is old and cunning and capable, he alone, of shifting as many hens as any four other foxes, you would not only be amazed, but you would declare it impossible. And that's where you would be wrong, for the thing happened at Prato, in this very country, in these

latter days, and if I can relate it to you
as nicely as it took place, I have no doubt
about making you laugh.   Anyhow, I'll try.

You know Santolo di Doppio del Quadro
for one of those who are hard to deceive.
He is a stoutish man with old-fashioned
whiskers.   He plays chess in his apron, and
does his own marketing.   People fancy he
is quite a simpleton, but beware of his shoe-
toe !   He knows his reckoning as well as
another, especially when he plays cards
with the ladies.   He is a man of sound conscience ; he would willingly help a widow
who was in need of the stuff for a petticoat
for a marriageable daughter, provided he
was paid back the value in yarn.   Taking
one year with another he weaves a good
deal of linen in his shop, and always has
plenty cf spinning to give out.   When he
comes unexpectedly among a group of women seated round a fire he plants himself
on the lowest stool and, if one of them
drops her spindle in the ashes, he picks it
up and hands it back with a low bow, and
then tells them some of the funniest tales
you ever heard.   He is a devotee of the
Virgin Mary, but withal a jolly fellow who
enjoys a joke and is slow to take offence.

This man therefore on hearing that one
of his friends was getting married, thought
at once of obstructing the wedding proces-
sion, as is the custom in this town, in order
to get something from the bride and then
to poke fun at the bridegroom, who was, he
too, a noble and gallant young man, accustomed all day long to take in others and to
get himself nicely caught in his turn. He
went off for one of his friends, one of those
fine fellows to whom one has only to say :
' Come,' and they come, and : ' Stay,' and
they stay ; being so little habituated to say
no, that before coming away with you no
matter where, if another arrives who wishes
to take him someplace else, simply while
you are getting your cloak, he will go, for
not knowing how to refuse. The most serviceable man in life ; if he says to one of
his comrades while playing at spotted cards:
' Give me the ace of denier,' and the comrade hands him thirty-two, he answers :
' All right.' Never angry, never grumbling,
never uttering an evil word, he would eat
without hunger, drink without thirst, fast
without there being any vigil, hear two
masses on a weekday and none on Sunday,
merely for company. To give pleasure, he

would sleep till midday or get up before
daybreak ; never eat salad in winter or
drink water in summer ; if you were sad he
would cheer you ; if you were gay he would
make your sides split with laughing ; he
would sooner spend money than earn it,
give than receive, oblige than ask.   When
he has cash, he spends it : when he has
none, he lives without spending that of others ; if he borrows, he gives back ; if he
lends, he forgets to claim it ; tell him the
truth, he believes it ; tell him lies, he holds
them for downright certainties ; he prefers
to think of nothing rather than puzzle his
brains and, what we must begrudge him, is
that he bears misfortune better than anyone else I know.   In fine, he is one of the
best, and born to please.

Santolo, having therefore met him, said
to him :   ' Fallabacchio, I want us to have
a bit of sport with the man who is marrying
Verdespina this evening.   I have found out
who will be with the bride, and the way
they will go.   I reckon we ought to get
enough out of them to regale ourselves on
two fat kids at their expense.   And we will
invite the bridegroom to the feast, and
have a bit of fun out of him, not half ! '

' Oh! yes, yes,' replied Fallabacchio, nodding his head and hugging Santolo, ' Oh ! we will buy two champion kids, and I will pick them myself. I will get two fat milk kids from Fagiuoli who understands such things. . I will make the sauce myself, and shall boil one of the hind quarters. I shall dress the civet with sweet majoram, and the kidneys with eggs. Oh, what a chance ! How we shall guttle ! To begin with, we shall eat the livers with pepper, but no laural, only sage ! ' And he jumped for joy, and added : ' We shall want something to drink ; where shall we go for the wine ? '

' You can leave that to me.'

' Come on then, let's get on the job.'

Thus chatting about the supper, they waited for tidings of the bride's setting out, and then rushed off before her. Racing away, wet with sweat, and hatless, they caught the cortege near the Torre degli Scrini. Those who were accompanying the bride, seeing them from afar, said to themselves : ' Here they come ; what shall we do ? ' The bride, quite young as you know, and in tears at the thought of leaving home, nevertheless kept her head and replied : ' Let them come, I shall satisfy then ; mother and I have thought out what to do.'

Santolo and Fallabacchio had at last got
up to them, and they cried out together :
' Give us a gratuity, or we shall not let you
pass,' and, as the folks made no reply, Fallabacchio shouted : ' If you do not give us
a gratuity I will run away with the bride
on my back.'

The bride's friends looked at one another
but kept silent. The chaste young bride,
whose tear-stained cheeks helped the illu-
sion, took a ring from her finger, not without much time and difficulty, and handed
it to the men, saying : ' Take this pledge
and, for God's sake, cause us no further
misfortunes ; but be on your guard not to
lose it, it is the finest ring I have.'

The merry fools, believing they had
caught a fine fish, gathered up their nets
and went off full of glee to Antonio dei Bardi's where there were, as every evening,
many gentlemen playing and otherwise
passing the time. They went in laughing
uproariously and kicking up such a dust as
never was, and intimating that they had
just performed some wonderful cleverness,
and showing the ring to any who would
look. These latter, whether they knew but

little about it, or to leave them in their
blissful ignorance, told them the brilliant
was a genuine one worth a pile of money,
and thus confirmed them in their first opinion. That their glory might be spread
throughout the whole world and the high
renown of so magnificent a result might be
raised above the clouds, our heroes resolved
to go that very night and make a display
of their trophy in the best houses of Prato
and to triumph publicly over it on the mor-
row in broad daylight.

They first visited Monna Amorrorisca, a
lovely and bewitching young woman, Fallabacchio's gossip and near kin to the bride.
There, with much mirth, they related the
adventure, and exhibited the ring at a dis-
tance, as people point to the Cintola. Everyone said : ' Bring it a bit nearer,' but
they exclaimed : ' Not likely ; do you want
us to lose it ? ' At length however they
let Monna Amorrorisca view it closely ; as
soon as she got hold of it, she discovered
that it had been fabricated at the expense
of an old candlestick, and that the stone
was quarried in the Glass Mountains. She
began to laugh and, after having kept them
some time on edge : ' By Gad ! ' she says to

them : 'guard it most preciously and take
care not to lose it ; you would ruin Verdespina.' 'The deuce ! and what is it worth,
in your opinion ?' asked Santolo. 'Indeed, the night is a bad time for valuing
jewels, especially when they are of great
worth, as this one is ; but, at a rough guess,
taking into account both brass and glass,
soldering, edging, and chasing, it is worth
not less than two farthings, perhaps three.'

Santolo, assuming his serious air and
snatching the ring out of her hands, cried :
'Oh, do you not see how she imposes on us ?'
But, when he had the ring in his hand, he
did not feel quite so sure of himself. He
perceived by its color and weight that he
had been to catch partridges with an ox,
and he began to puff and blow.

'What is the matter with you ?' asked
Fallabacchio. 'Do you not see how she is
jeering at us ? Bitch ! what a beautiful
ruby ! What is this I say ? It is a corne-
lian, no, a turquoise. Anyhow, whatever
it is, it is superb. I will go straight away
to a goldsmith and raise a florin on it so
that we can buy the kids for the day after
to-morrow. What day will it fall on ? It
will be Saturday—they will be fat.'

Without further parley, off he went to a goldsmith's shop and assured himself that the ring might be a suitable present for a nursemaid, at a pinch. The two friends were furious at being duped, and they swore that they would plunder the bride's trousseau and demand double value for everything they could capture, before giving it up. However, the bridegroom heard of their threats, and he arranged that some of his friends should keep the two jokers out of the way until all the thing were safely packed away, and thus they were fooled again.

But Verdespina, ill satisfied because the joke was not carried further, made her intentions known to Monna Amorrorisca, and the latter, highly delighted, prepared beforehand what was to be done.

On Saturday morning Verdespina sent word to Santolo and Fallabacchio that they were to return her ring, that she would give them a gratuity, and so generous a one too that they would be able to treat themselves to a couple of kids. The fellows would have willingly believed that she wanted to make a laughing-stock of them if certain folks, who had been given the hint, had not

thought of whispering in their ears that
Monna Amorrorisca had changed their ring,
that they' knew for certain that it was
worth more than thirty crowns, and that
the bridegroom was wild when he heard the
story and intended to put to put a stop to
the game at once. And, believe me, they
swallowed the tale !

They went to the gossip and asked her if
she had changed the ring. She first took
to laughing and, while laughing, to deny
it with those looks which people assume
when they want to jest in saying no ; they
were only the more certain that the gossip
had changed it and, getting very angry,
cried out ' robber' and almost called her
names—how she had them mocked by the
whole town, how folks did not act in that
manner, and how she must give them back
the ring or take the consequences. But to
irritate them still more, she held her tongue.
Fallabacchio, raising his voice higher, cried :
' Gossip, give us the ring ; if not, I swear I
will snatch your watch off you when you
are at church to-morrow.'

Seeing that things were going as she wished, but pretending to be affronted, Monna
Amorrorisca told them she had not changed

the ring to wrong them, still less to keep it,
as they seemed to think, but simply to
laugh over it a day or two with them, then
to give it back to them. Now, since they
had got angry, since they threatened her
and made such a fuss about it, she intended
to treat them as they deserved. Conse-
quently, let them not think to get back the
ring unless they first pay down for two kids,
and the fattest that could be found in the
market this morning. Santolo and Fallabacchio, seeing her in such a rage, wished
to pacify her, but all to no purpose. She
left them to fight it out together and flung
off, saying :   ' Now remember what I have
told you ! '

The two fellows walked out quite down-
hearted and pondering on what to do. At
the same moment, the bridegroom sent
them word that he must have the ring at
all costs, and they could ask whatever
they liked. He wanted the matter settled
at once as the joke had gone too far for his
liking. Fallabacchio turned to Santolo :
' The bridegroom is within his rights, but
what the devil can we do ? Let us buy the
kids for the gossip, we can ask her to supper at the same time and make peace with

her. Then if the bridegroom wants his
ring he must pay for it, otherwise he gets
nothing.'

They stuck to this resolution, went to
the market, bought two fat kids, took them
to the gossip and asked for the ring. She
told them that she would not fail to give it
them, but not till Sunday evening, when
they must come to her house and share in
the feast. What she was doing with them
was, said she, for their good, because she
wished also to invite Verdespina and her
husband who, in this way, would feel less
disinclination to settle with them generous-
ly. They told her this was a good idea but
that she ought to send word previously to
the husband to leave them alone and not
reclaim the ring before the following evening. As to that, they might leave it to her,
replied she, for she knew quite well how to
pacify the husband.

The poor dupes having departed, Monna
Amorrorisca sent word to Verdespina that
everything was ready for the unravelling of
the plot, and that she and her husband
were to come to her house to-morrow evening. Verdespina replied that they would
be there without fail.

On Sunday evening Monna Amorrorisco invited a number of girl friends and their husbands to her party, so that the joke might get discussed all over the town, and also that homage might be paid to the new-made bride. Of course, Santolo and Falla-bacchio were there.

The supper over, Monna Amorrorisca and Verdespina, desiring that nobody should ignore the joke played on Santolo and Fallabacchio and that the men should be thoroughly mocked, related what had taken place ; men and women, all, all began to set up a clatter at the expense of the two fellows who at first seemed inclined to kick up a dust ; but, seeing that the more they defended themselves the more they were laughed at, like good-natured fellows they joined in the general merriment, stating that after all it was not any miracle that they were mistaken about the value of the ring as they were not goldsmiths. But some say that Santolo did not laugh very heartily ; being more thoroughly duped than Fallabacchio, he took more of it to his own account.

ROMANCE IX

The Even Match

You must know there was at Siena, in
the Camporeggi quarter (the time is not so
far back but that everyone of you will remember it), a certain Monna Francesca of
a pretty good family and fairly well off.
She had remained widow with one daughter
already ripe for marriage (in fact she got
her married a few months after to a certain
Meo di Mino da Rossia who, being occupied
in the management of the magnificent Bor-
ghes' demesnes, lived most of the time outside Siena) and a son who was scarcely sev-
en years old. Being busy in bringing up
her two children and unwilling to marry
again, she lived very quietly. In the mean-
time, a Dominican Brother, a bachelor of

theology named Fra Timoteo, seeing she
was fresh and goodlooking, cast his eyes
upon her. Either because of the severe
flagellations which he administered to himself, or because of the prolonged fastings to
which he was subjected, his face shone to
such a degree that you could have lighted
a match on his ruddy cheeks.

The good lady thought he would be just
the man for her, one who would suit her
quiet situation and help her to remedy the
irksome privations of widowhood. Now,
whether it was from him or from her that
the first advances came, I really cannot say;
let it suffice for you that she became a near
kin to the good Lord, and she went to confession so often, and stayed so willingly at
the San Domenico Church, that the people
of the district proclaimed her a half saint.

While things were going on as you have
just heard, the daughter, Laura by name,
had long since divined her mother's wisdom
by many signs and, unwilling to belie that
elegant proverb 'What is the offspring of
the hen, must scratch the dunghill,' resolved to follow her example. Soon did she
prove so apt a pupil that, what time her
mother was displaying her conscience to the

pious monk, she was learning from a certain Andreuolo Pannili, a lawyer, the conduct to be observed in the consummation
of matrimony.

Now it happened that one night when
the widow was entertaining her spiritual
comforter in her room, that they made
more noise than was wise and the daughter
divined the nature of their devotions.   Believing now that she herself need take no
further precautions, she sent her brother to
fetch their neighbor Agnesa, a friend of all
true lovers, and asked her to bid her sweet-
·heart come at once.   The gentleman lost
no time in putting in an appearance and,
entering her room by the usual way, laid
himself down by his darling in bed ; but
Laura, instead of arranging it so that her
mother could not hear them, began to car-
ess her lover quite as if he were her husband, while saying as loudly as possible :
' O my dear soul, you are a thousand times
welcome !   O my sweet fresh cheeks, my
ruby lips, when shall I kiss you enough so
as to grow weary of it, I will not say satia-
ted !   Never, surely never, were I to kiss
you till I died ! '   In pronouncing these
words she gave him such smacks that you

might have heard them a mile away. The
lawyer being made acquainted with what
was up, he too did not fail to do his duty,
and there finally resulted such a commotion
as made Monna Francesca's ears tingle.
Attracted by the noise, she tip-toed to their
door and ascertained that they were not
confining their activities to mere words.
Like many another woman who busies herself with the faults of others rather than
her own, she grew angry beyond all bounds
and, driving the door in before her with
unparalleled fury, she bounced into the
room, found Laura in bed, affronted her in .
such a manner that you would have said
she was going to eat her up raw. Foaming
with rage, she squawked out: ' Tell me,
what's that I've just been hearing you say ?
O Laura, Laura, is this the way, is this the
way virtuous girls behave ? Have I taught
you these things ? Have I brought you up
in this way ? Have I grounded you in such
principles that you durst hurl this insult
into my face ? Have I ever set you such
an example ? O God ! whom do you take
after ? O my husband ! how fortunate
that you died and have been spared this
shame ! What will our relations say—what

will your husband say, he who dotes on you so ? You might at least have avoided such goings-on in my house, and have waited till your husband took you away, as he intends to do shortly. Away, slut, away, get out of my sight; you are no daughter of mine, you brazen-faced bitch ! O God, I might have suspected this, had I not been blind ! But alas, how could I have thought such a thing of a daughter of mine, when here at this moment, though I have seen with my own eyes, I cannot believe it. O God, my too ardent affection for Thee, the too great confidence I had, knowing my own life, caused me to see all awry. Now I understand why, the other morning at church, Monna Andreoccia warned me agaist letting you gad about : she knew something, and it only wanted this to make us the talk of the town ! There then is the reason for your secret talks with that Agnesa, yes, there it is, but I'll pay you out, my lady ! Have I not given you a young and vigorous husband, good enough for anybody ? Just you wait till he gets back; I will tell him myself what you have been doing, and he shall chastise you with his own hand.'

While uttering these threats and many

more besides, she made as big a row as an
old dame would who had lost a pen of poul-
try. Laura, who, all the while her mother
was snubbing her, had remained with her
eyes fixed on the ground, as one wholly
confused, pretending to be greatly afraid,
answered her: 'My dear little mamma, I
accuse myself before you for having done
evil, and beg pardon for God's sake; I beseech you to excuse my youth, to have at
the same time respect for mine honor and
your own, to be good enough to forgive me
this time, and to say nothing to my husband; I swear to you on my love for him,
never more to do the slightest thing against
your wish. This time, that God may forgive me my grievous sin, that He may with-
draw me from the gates of hell and remove
this thorn from my tortured flesh, I wish
to make a full confession before going to
sleep again. Be therefore kind enough to
go to your room and fetch me that holy
monk whom you are keeping locked up;
he it is shall give me absolution.'

Consider how the mother felt when she
heard this request, and whether she regret-
ted she had made such a fuss about a fault
of which she was now herself convicted.

At the moment when, wishing to hide her confusion, she began to mutter I know not what philastrocoles altogether beside the point, it seemed to Andreuolo that now was the time to come from behind the curtain and handle the matter in legal style. So he burst in on them, saying : 'Monna Francesca, what is the use of all these exclamations ? If you have discovered your daughter with a young man, she has caught you with a monk ; you are both at the same game—six to one and half-a-dozen to the other. The best thing you can do is to get back to your monk, while I stay here with Laura, and then we shall, all four of us, enjoy our love in holy accord. We shall be so cautious that no one will ever be the wiser, whereas if you do as you say, you will throw so much meat on the fire that more than one batch of wood will be needed to cook it, and you will be the first to repent. Be wise ; take the safe road while you can, and give yourself no cause for sorrow.' The poor widow knew not what to say, she was so abashed. She wanted to steal away without further parley. At last, feeling that she had only heard the truth, she muttered : ' All right, I will

say no more, except that you do as you like.
And I beseech you, young man, let there
be no scandal.' Having said these words
she returned to her room. But the young
man followed her and compelled her to
agree to prepare a supper for them all that
very night, and acknowledge one another
as relations, and arrange that each might
come to the house whenever he liked without fear of interference. The holy concord
worked so well that the two women were
daily more contented. It is true, indeed,
that sometimes in the morning while talking together of their lovers' exploits, they
discovered that very often the young man
had allowed himself to be surpassed, and
that by more than one affray, by the monk,
although the latter was growing old. This
made Laura envious of her mother, and was
the cause of many quarrels with Andreuolo.

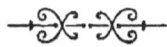

ROMANCE X

The Will

You must know that we meet in all professions far fewer upright men than sordid men; you will not then find it very strange that there are among monks but a small number near that perfection which their rule imposes on them, and that moreover Avarice, which reigns over all courts, both spiritual and temporal, has claimed a little corner within the cloisters of poor friars.

There was at Novara, a city of Lombardy, a very rich lady named Madonna Agnesa who was left a widow through the death of one Gaudenzio. He had left her, besides her marriage portion, which, according to the customs of these realms, was considerable, immence riches, investing her with their entire free disposal on the condition that, without marrying again, she should attend to the education of the four sons he had by her.

Gaudenzio was hardly dead when news of the will reached the Father of the Monastery of the Brothers of Santo Nazaro, as he kept a look-out for this sort of thing. His office was to see that no pretty widow should escape them, but should gird on the cord of the blessed Saint Francis, and that, becoming one of their beguines, listening daily to their sermons, begging their prayers for her dead, she might address to them in return nice pies in the Lombardy style; then that she should, in process of time, being inflamed with burning zeal for the pious works of the blessed Fra Ginepro or some other of their saints, decide about founding in their Church a chapel where they painted funny stories—such as when Saint Francis was preaching to the birds in the desert, when he made the miraculous soup or when the angel Gabriel brought him his sandals; all she needed to do after that was to endow it with a nice round sum that they might be able to celebrate every year the feast of those blessed Stigmata, possessed of so

many virtues, Lord my God ! and to recite
an office every Monday for the souls of her
relations detained in the pains of purgatory.
But for the simple reason that they cannot,
owing to their profession of poverty, hold
so much wealth as belonging to the monastery, they have lately devised a scheme of
possessing it as chapel endowments, and
they think perhaps by this means to cheat
Our Lord in the same way as they daily
cheat men. They delude themselves that
God does not see the depths of their intentions and knows not that, if they act thus,
it is because they are envious and jealous
of those gorbellied monks who, far from
wandering barefooted, carry with them five
pairs of pumps, and do nothing but mug
themselves in luxurious cells ; who, if they
are perchance obliged to go outside the
monastery, jog along at their ease on a fat
pony, and who do not tire their minds with
books, for fear the science they might glean
therein might elate them with pride and
cause them to fall away from the monastic
simplicity.

To return to the point, this devout Fath-
er-guardian scented out the widow so well
and made such a spluther round her with

his sandals that she consented to become
affiliated to the Third Order, and the monks
got many good meals and new habits out
of her. This seemed to them as yet nothing or scarcely worth while, and they
were all day long at her heels, reminding
her of the article for the chapel. But the
good lady, both because she knew she would
be doing wrong by robbing her sons to bestow on the monks, and because she was
naturally mean, went no farther than promises.

While they were incessantly soliciting her
and she feeding them on hopes, it happened
that she fell dangerously ill and sent for
the father, Fra Serafino, to hear her confession. He ran to her with all speed and,
as soon as he had heard her coufession, seeing that the vintage-time had at last arrived, he told her, as an act of charity, that
she should think of her salvation while
there was yet time; that she should not
rely upon her sons, who were only awaiting
her death to laugh at her; and that she
should recall to mind Donna Lionora Cac-
cia, the wife of Doctor Cervagio, that when
she was dead there was not one of her sons
who was willing to light a candle for her,

not even on All Souls' Day ; that this was
very little for one so rich as she, and that
both she and her relations would gain from
her bequests. In short, he told the tale so
well that the dying woman was almost resolved to say she would, and asked him to
come back next day when he should have
h r decision. Meanwhile, her youngest son,
Agabio, having got a hint of what was up,
told his brothers, and they, to make quite
sure, thought it would be well, should the
monk return, if one of them hid under the
bed and listened to the arrangement. So
on the next day, Fra Serafino having come
back to conclude the bargain, Agabio slipped under his mother's bed and heard the
monk urge her so forcibly, unfold to her so
many arguments, quote so many doctors
and put her into such a fright about Purgatory, that she resolved to bequeath two
hundred pounds in hard cash to build and
decorate a chapel, a hundred more for altar
ornaments and, as a donation, (provided
that a feast should be celebrated in it every
year, and a mass said daily) the half of an
undivided demesne which she owned at
Camigliano, near the pillory, which was
worth in all more than three thousand

pounds. Having agreed upon the name of
the chapel and the services, the monk hurried off, and Agabio got from under the bed
without his mother's perceiving it, and related what he had heard to his brothers
who, aided by a few relations, came to their
mother and dissuaded her from such a plan.

Agabio, feeling that his mother would be
satisfied to let the stream follow its natural
course, thought it would be as well to get a
laugh out of the Father; he called aside
one of their footmen and despatched him
on his mother's part to bid the monk come
no more to the house to tire her and talk
over again what was settled—her sons had
got to know of her scheme and had planned
to play him an ugly trick, should he re-ap-
pear. Let him nevertheless remain tran-
quil—she would take care that her wishes
were carried out. From the moment he
should learn that Our Lord had disposed of
her, he had only to go to Ser Tomeno Al-
zalendina's and ask for the will and get it
executed.

The footman went and delivered the mes-
sage, so that Fra Serafino appeared no more;
but, having soon learnt that Madonna Agnesa had yielded her soul to her Maker, he

quickly went to Ser Tomeno and asked for
the will. Ser Tomeno, advised beforehand
by Agabio of what he was to do, answered
him unhesitatingly that he must see Agabio
who was acquainted with the provisions of
the will. Without more ado the monk
called on Agabio and, after the usual expressions of sympathy, asked to see the
will. Agabio made no other reply to his
request except that he was greatly surprised to see him enquiring for what did not
concern him, and told him to mind his own
business. The good Father did not in any
way trouble himself about this reception ;
he believed all the more that the will was
only the more favorable to him, and without further argument betook himself to a
certain Master Niccolo, attorney for the
monastery, and asked him to deal with this
affair. Niccolo at once had Ser Tomeno
summoned before the Bishop's vicar, and
demanded a copy of the will. Tomeno,
having received the summons, ran off to
Agabio and told him how things stood.
Agabio, who was only waiting for that, repaired to the vicar, who was a great friend
of his, and informed him of all that had
taken place up to then, as well as of what

he intended to do, always providing it had
his approval. The vicar, being of course
the monk's enemy, in his capacity of priest,
assured him that he would be very glad of
it ; and so the next day there came Fra
Serafino and his attorney demanding that
they should be shown a copy of the will.

Agabio stepped forward at this request
and said : 'My Lord Vicar, I am very happy to produce it in the presence of your
Lordship ; but on the condition that all its
clauses be executed in good and due form,
by all those named therein, no matter who.'

'The thing is clear,' replies the vicar ;
'the law disposes that he who has the prof-
its ought also to bear the charges. Produce therefore the will ; justice will have it
so.' Agabio, immediately pulling a large
roll of paper from his pocket, handed it to
a notary of the bench, telling him to read
it, which he did.

After having read the appointing of heirs
and a few other legacies mentioned in order
to inspire greater confidence in the guest,
the notary came at length to the part con-
cerning the monk and which began thus :
'ITEM—for the safeguard of my chi'drens'
goods and the salvation of all the widows

of Novara, I wish that by these same children and their own hands, there be given
to Fra Serafino, at present Guardian of the
Convent of San Nazaro, fifty lashes, the
best and heaviest they shall know how to
apply, so that this monk and his equals
may long remember that it is not always
advisable to wish to persuade silly women
without judgment and foolish bigots to dis-
inherit and ruin their children for the sake
of enriching chapels.' Such bursts of laugh-
ter arose from all parts of the court that
the notary could not finish his reading, and
do not ask me if all those present began to
make a fool of the poor Father who, seeing
himself stuck there with shame and affront,
wished to get off back to the convent and
draw up a complaint to be sent to the Ap-
ostolic See. But Agabio, seizing him by
the habit and holding him fast, began to
cry out : ' Hold on, Father, whither away
so fast ? I am quite prepared to carry out
the duties imposed on me by the will,' and
turning towards the Vicar, without letting
go of the monk, he added : ' My Lord, have
him stretched on the rack—I am bent on
fulfilling my obligation ; otherwise, I shall
complain of your Lordship and say you

have not rendered me justice.' The vicar thought this was enough, if not too much, considering, as he ought, the dignity of the monk and the Order of Minor Friars; he turned to Agabio and, half laughing, said: 'Agabio, sufficient that you have shown your good will; Fra Serafino, opining that this legacy would be burthensome on the convent, refuses to accept it; since he refuses, you cannot force it on him. Let him therefore go about his business.' And, with the kindest words he could find, he dismissed him.

The monk, as soon as he got leave, went full of rage to the convent, and remained therein a long while without showing his nose, owing to his great shame. He never again exhorted widows to bequeath their goods to chapels, especially if they had grown-up sons capable of holding him up to ridicule. Yet, the vicar had to repent of it—the joke cost him more than five hundred florins.

END

CONTENTS

Printed in France by Ch. Unsinger, 83, rue du Bac, Paris